THE
TENEMENT

By Barrett J. Bilotta

Harvard Book Store
Cambridge, MA

Published at Harvard Book Store
Cambridge, MA

ISBN: 9780984883738

www.thebostontrilogy.com

CONTENTS

THE
TENEMENT

1

A DAY IN THE LIFE
BOSTON, 1960

Below the high brick walls of the Boston Garden, home of the Celtics and the Bruins, lies the West End, a hundred-year-old immigrant neighborhood with narrow winding streets and three-decker tenement buildings. In 1960, the West End's residents made up an immigrant stew of mostly Italians, seasoned well with Polish, Jewish, Irish, African, and Ukrainian Americans.

Not far away in Boston's downtown Market Square, the narrow streets fanned out to the west into the peninsula that was the West End. Over the Square, the elevated Green Line train wound its way to the north, crossing the river to Chelsea and beyond, and to the south, rattling back into the underground and under the posh sections of Beacon Hill. Beyond Beacon Hill lay the Massachusetts State Capitol with its gold dome and the Boston Common.

The West End was an isolated neighborhood, a place between the Harbor and the working docks, a place where Americans first came, and often never left. But things were changing...

On a September day, a truck from the City of Boston pulled to a stop. Workmen jumped out and quickly propped up a large wooden sign. Passersby from the West End gathered and stared at the billboard of downtown Boston in panoramic perspective—the harbor in the fore-ground, the docks and financial district dominating the few remaining downtown neighborhoods, among them the West End, outlined bold-ly in red. Over the scene, a painted banner proclaimed: *River Run—Planning with the People.*

Among the curious onlookers stood Eddie Sveglio, an Italian-American man in his early twenties. He had dark brown hair that was wavy and short. Eddie's face was square, and his sharp, dark features reflected a keen mind. His body was taut and well-proportioned. He was over six feet tall.

Eddie had grown up in the West End. He craned his head and tried to see what all the fuss was about. Why were TV crews setting up their cameras? Why were the *Boston Globe* and *Herald* here, of all places? He squinted his deep brown eyes at the modular blocks of apartments in the painted city that was a revision of the West End, this River Run. What were once twenty-odd acres of three-decker's and squat brick commer-cial buildings, now appeared in the painting as a landscaped office park of separated glass cubes, decorated with tropical-looking shrubs. Eddie smiled. He could see those shrubs after a Boston winter.

City of Boston cars arrived and a small mob of dignitaries hud-dled in front of the sign. The City officials gathered around a table that held an architectural model of the redevelopment scheme, all under a clear plastic bubble.

Next to Eddie stood Joseph Lazzaro, a stocky man well into his seventies, his hair silvered, his face creased with sun-baked wrinkles. Together they stood on the edge of a crowd of journalists and TV cameras.

"Can you believe this?" Eddie asked Mr. Lazzaro. "This is purely a show for the press. The Mayor and his gang don't give a hoot what we think down here."

Mr. Lazzaro smiled gently. "Now, Eddie, let's hear them out," he said. "Look, over there, Joe Angelino, your old school buddy. You know, Angel."

"Angel?"

"Over there in the suit."

"What in the world is he doing here? I thought he was still at Harvard," Eddie said.

"Shhh..." Mr. Lazzaro whispered back.

News photographers snapped pictures, bulbs flashed, and cam-era crews began filming. The chief administrator for the City, Edward

O'Mally, a distinguished-looking Irishman in his early forties, called the group to order. Next to him was affable Mayor Cowley, recent victim of a minor stroke, propped up in a wheelchair. Nearly fifty, he still exuded the charm of a curly-headed parochial choirboy.

"Many of you must be wondering why the Mayor called today's press conference," O'Mally said. "I know this has been rather sudden, but there's good reason to be here today on this important spot—Market Square, the famous gateway to the West End."

More flash bulbs popped and O'Mally paused as a Green Line trolley rolled overhead.

"As you know, for the past eight years, we have been seeking federal approval and funds for clearance and redevelopment of the West End. Today I have the pleasure of announcing that the Federal Government has given us the definitive go-ahead. There's no more waiting. Work can go forward at a measured pace that fits the needs of the city and the West End's citizens."

Flash bulbs went off by the dozen as O'Mally's hand swept over the scaled down model of the city. A newsman from the *Globe* shouted, "Mr. O'Mally...," while his competitor from the *Herald* chimed in with, "Sir, what is the next step in the urban renewal? Is it for real this time?"

O'Mally flashed a wide, confident smile and held up his hands. "Now, I'm not finished. Hold on. Let me continue. There will be plenty of time for questions later. As you can see on the table, we have a model of the new West End, River Run. This replica covers a thirty-eight acre area. These attractive high-rises will house twenty-four-hundred apartments. Nearby on the Charles River there will be a handful of townhouses. All the old tenement buildings will be destroyed. However, three buildings will be preserved: the museum, the library and the Holy Name Church. According to our schedule, total clearance of the West End's older housing should be accomplished within three years, by the spring of 1964. By that time no one will ever know that this struggling, and often stricken, urban area ever existed."

O'Mally smiled and turned to the Mayor. "Now, I believe the Mayor has a few words. Mr. Mayor..."

A crowd of locals had joined Eddie and Mr. Lazzaro. They buzzed with confusion.

"Do these idiots know where they are?" Eddie asked the people around him. "Saying that right down here in our faces. They want to get in front of the cameras."

9

The Mayor grappled with the microphone and sent out several electronic squeals. "Thank you, Mr. O'Mally," the Mayor said. "I cannot emphasize enough how important these new high-rises will be for the city of Boston. They will bring in additional municipal income, which the city badly needs. They will also add quality shoppers to our downtown area. This should increase the morale of private investors and, hopefully, this will trigger a spiral of private rebuilding in our city. I want to add that the West End is being redeveloped not only for the good of the city but for the sake of the residents as well."

"How's that, Mr. Mayor?" Eddie yelled over the heads of the journalists, who all now turned to stare in his direction.

The Mayor looked quickly at Eddie and smiled. "I'll get to that, son."

The police detachment of a dozen officers watched Eddie and the crowd growing around the press circle.

Continuing, the Mayor declared, "Over the years, both private and public agencies have conducted studies, which conclude that the area is indeed in a deprived state. "I might add that the local settlement landlords and the Catholic Archdiocese have long supported our redevelopment efforts."

A wise-looking priest in the line of officials nodded in approval.

"Who's that priest?" Eddie asked Mr. Lazzaro.

"I'm not sure," Mr. Lazzaro replied, squinting at the cleric. "He's probably with the Archbishop's Office. Take it easy. This is just for show. You'll see. We've been hearing this talk for years."

"I don't like the feeling here," Eddie said.

"And in our efforts to plan a careful and socially acceptable transition for the people of the West End," the Mayor said, "we've consulted with major universities." The microphone system squealed with feedback. The Mayor rolled his wheelchair back slightly and smiled. "In fact, we will have a transition site office right here in the West End during the entire process. A team of specialists will be available to smooth out any bumps caused by the changeover. Their leader will be Mr. Joseph Angelino, a former resident of the West End, and now a graduate student at Harvard's Urban Planning Department. Mr. Angelino has been chosen to head that site office and will be on the job this fall. Mr. Angelino..."

Joe "Angel" Angelino, looking trim and fresh in his pinstriped suit, stepped forward slightly and waved at the cameras. He looked confident and older than his years; his black hair was cropped close, and his teeth were dazzling white. He smiled at the television cameras and waved good-naturedly to the crowd. His tall frame and athletic body made him appear powerful and in control.

"Mr. Angelino knows the West End's people well," the Mayor said, "which will be most helpful in accomplishing a good transition. Now, before I open the floor for questions, let me say that the toughest part of the urban renewal process is behind us. The danger now is moving too slowly. We must and will move ahead with vigor and persistence to reach a successful beautification. Now I'll be glad to take a few questions from the press."

Eddie paid little attention to the questions. He kept looking at Angel. They had grown up in the same tenement together, played basketball, starred as forwards in high school. They had been in the state finals together. And here Angel was, after being the good scholar, here he was serving the blood-sucking ghouls down at City Hall. Angel saw Eddie staring at him and nodded in his direction.

"You haven't answered my question, Mr. Mayor!" Eddie shouted. "How's this gonna help us, the residents of the West End?"

"Yeah!" came a cry of agreement from other residents.

"You'll have access to the housing, you'll have better choices than you have now," the Mayor said.

The crowd began booing him. From somewhere, a paper cup flew through the air. Other residents began shouting angry questions in the direction of the Mayor and his staff. The Mayor shook his head and threw up his hands. Police rolled him down the ramp to the entourage of City cars.

Eddie cut off Angel's retreat. "Hey, Angel, wait up." he called out, grabbing Angel by the sleeve. They were the same height and build.

"Hi Eddie, long time no see." Angel smiled and shook Eddie's hand.

"Hey, what's going on?" Eddie asked, still firmly holding on to Angel's hand. "You can't be serious."

"You heard the Mayor. It's a reality now. I'm going to do all I can to make the transition a smooth one."

"Forget that, okay? You go off to Harvard and come back to bulldoze the neighborhood? What? Where's your loyalty?"

"Hey now..." Angel finally pulled his hand from Eddie's tight grip. He stared at Eddie hard. "This has been in the works since we were in junior high. Remember the first time we heard about this from Father O'Donnell, when we were on that retreat in the eighth grade?"

11

"So what?" Eddie said. "Why do *you* have to join them?"

"This is no us-versus-them thing, Eddie."

"You better rethink your position. Maybe there's some other project at Harvard, maybe you could bulldoze the big shot WASPs off Brattle Street, you know, something really socially uplifting."

Angel, his face coloring slightly, studied Eddie. "Look, don't make this any harder than it has to be. Take my advice."

"Hear me good and hear me now," Eddie said. "I don't give a crap about your career. You've been suckered, you've crossed the Charles River and now you're back to do us in."

A few feet away, Mr. Lazzaro, who had been watching the two young men's interaction, sensed the tension building between them. These were the two little boys who had grown up together in his tenement building. He knew them well.

Mr. Lazzaro walked over and placed his hand on Eddie's shoulder. "Okay, Eddie, you've said your peace. This is not the place. Hi, Angel, how ya doing?"

"Hi, Mr. Lazzaro, I'm doing just fine. How about you?"

"Okay, but this is bad news for us," Mr. Lazzaro said. "We're not ready for this. I'm like Eddie. I'm surprised. It's all so sudden."

"It hasn't really been sudden. I was just telling Eddie, we've been hearing about this since the eighth grade. Look, we'll have plenty of time to discuss this," Angel said. "I'll be seeing you soon."

"Your limo's waiting," Eddie said. "You wouldn't want to keep the Mayor waiting, would you?" Eddie gave Angel a small push on the arm.

"Hey, Eddie," Angel said, shaking his head. "Knock it off."

"Don't," Mr. Lazzaro said to Eddie, pulling him by the arm. A heavyset cop watched them and frowned.

"No, I'm not gonna hurt you," Eddie said. "I just wanted to give you something from the old neighborhood...you know, a little human touch." Eddie grasped Angel's hand in a handshake and squeezed hard, but Angel didn't yield. Eddie grumbled under his breath, "Something to remember us by. We'll see you around, *paisano!*"

2

HAIRCUT

Eddie stepped off the Green Line train and followed the crowd down the metal stairs into the West End. He walked down the street half a block to Gino's Barbershop, where he stepped into aromas from his childhood—of hair tonic, talc powder, cigar smoke, and cigarettes. A spontaneous smile came upon Eddie's face. These familiar smells triggered memories from long ago of Saturday early morning haircuts.

Eddie nodded to the half dozen occupants of the barbershop, most of them retired Italian businessmen, now benched and passing the time from their favorite waiting room chairs. Presently, all eyes were affixed upon Sal, who was holding court. Sal had been retired from the grocery store business for nearly ten years and ever since, had made a stop at the barbershop a part of his daily routine.

Eddie slipped into an empty barber chair and lay back. "Just a trim today," Eddie said to Gino.

Gino was a portly man in his fifties whose long, graying sideburns were grown to make up for his bald head.

"So how's the job?" Gino asked. Gino eased back on the shears along the sides and just edged Eddie's thick hair.

"It's okay. Just another job, a warehouse thing, it puts bread on the table. Sort of...," Eddie replied. He looked out the window as a trucker unloaded red buckets of carnations onto the curb. On neighboring

Lindburgh Street, where women shopped for their fresh fruits and vegetables, delivery trucks double-parked, continuing to unload their produce into street stalls.

"So, today a holiday?" Gino asked.

"I took off early," Eddie said.

"You should become a barber like me. Steady work, you take orders from no one," Gino said, clipping a particularly stubborn strand of curly brown hair.

"Yeah, you got it made," Eddie acknowledged.

"Have you seen this morning's paper?" Gino asked Eddie.

"No...why?"

Gino grabbed a *Globe* from the counter and snapped it open to page one. "The Feds and Mayor Cowley, the thief. Here's the big deal announcement from yesterday. You think they're really gonna tear down the neighborhood?"

"I don't know," Eddie said, scanning the article, alongside a photo of a group picture showing Angel standing next to the Mayor.

"That Angel, I can't believe he's mixed up in this," Gino said. "You still talk with him?"

"No...well yesterday I did. He makes me feel like I've been away a long time," Eddie said and dropped the paper. "I feel like I'm just coming to my senses. I've been busy working, you know how you get."

How could this be a real threat? People had been worrying about this since he was a little kid, Eddie thought to himself.

Gino's cousin Vincenzo, a rickety old man in his eighties, said in his cracked, falsetto voice, "What's this bull?"

"What nerve, calling this place deprived," Gino retorted, stepping on the paper and the Mayor's photo.

"Hey, don't believe what you read in the paper." Sal said. "I've been retired, what, ten years from the grocery business. Gotta be fifteen years already they've been giving us headlines."

Vincenzo clacked his false teeth and leaned toward Eddie. "They're going to do it, they're not going to do it. They can't do nothin' right downtown. It's hogwash, I tell ya."

Carl, a bald man in his seventies, put down his *Field & Stream* and said in a measured voice, "It's just another attempt to scare us."

"Yeah, probably just another false alarm," Eddie agreed. "Don't get worked up."

Gino brushed Eddie's collar and powdered his neck.

14

"I don't care what they say. They'll never knock down our West End," Gino said whipping off the striped apron from Eddie. "There, good as new. What a handsome fella, eh?"

"Thanks Gino," Eddie said. He slipped him two quarters and headed for the door. "You guys don't work too hard." Eddie hung in the doorway and looked back at the gang of elders. "Oh, ah, tonight's my daughter's birthday, one year old. You guys want to stop by? I know you got a busy social calendar."

"Ciao," they said and waved him out the door.

"Hey," Gino said to Eddie, "no matter what, you give both your ladies a big kiss from me and the guys, okay?"

"He's a good boy," Vincenzo said. "I knew his father and grandfather."

"When did he get married?" Carl asked looking at Vincenzo.

"Get back to your trout fishing," Vincenzo said. "I can't remember my way to the toilet, what do I know?"

Everyone laughed.

"Yeah, that's the way it is now," Carl said.

Eddie checked his watch and headed down to The Club. Outside the entrance he rang the doorbell. A panel slid open revealing a bloodshot eye.

"It's Eddie," a familiar gruff voice said. The door swung open and revealed Buddy, a heavyset man in his thirties with a flattop haircut.

"Hi Eddie."

"Is Mario in there?" Eddie asked.

"Yeah, he's in the back playing cards. Better get to him before he needs to borrow more of your money!" Buddy said, slapping Eddie on the back. Eddie headed down the dark hallway. It smelled vaguely of old beer and floor polish. He rang another doorbell, waited, and with a solid pneumatic swish, a red padded door opened.

Before him lay several green baize tables covered with racing forms. Alfredo, the resident West End bookie, nodded his head and smiled around a mouth of yellow rabbity teeth. He talked on the phone while a cigarette hung from his mouth. He jotted down bets on combustible flash paper for the next race.

Eddie went over to the card table where Mario was playing poker with a bunch of the locals. He pulled up a chair next to Mario. The radio was on, the Sox and the Orioles.

15

"Hey Eddie," Mario said.

"How's your luck?" Eddie asked.

"I'm ahead about fifty," Mario replied and turned to baldheaded Carlo, the dealer. "Give me three." He looked at Eddie's haircut closely. "What? Are you Errol Flynn joining the Marines or something?" He peeled his cards open. "I'll bet a fin."

Pat, the local baker, had stopped in for a hand. Beside him was a cake box. The other players, Carlo and Johnnie, were well known to Eddie as habitués of the dark cool clubhouse, day or night. They went around calling and betting.

"I call," Johnnie said.

"Three jacks!" Mario exclaimed as he tossed down his cards.

"Got me, again!" Carlo said. "What an ass! I should've folded."

"Have a heart, Pretty Boy," said Pat.

"Sorry guys." Mario smiled and cocked an ear to the radio. "Hey, hear that?"

"What?" Carlo said.

"It's Ted Williams. This could be his last time at the plate here," Eddie said. "Listen to that crowd."

Alfredo, turned up the volume and the crowd continued roaring.

The announcer was excited. "Listen to that crowd," he said. "They're all on their feet. It's such a strange sight. The lights have been on since the sixth inning on this cold, overcast New England day."

"What are the odds, Alfredo?" Mario asked. "That he'll hit a home run?"

Eddie looked at Alfredo, who paused to consult a scrap of paper. Alfredo was of indeterminate age, smoked into a permanent state of preservation, too many years in the dark cave. Eddie wasn't sure he had ever seen Alfredo outside in the daylight. Maybe once at Don Brindisi's funeral, years ago.

"He ain't had it the three previous at bats," Alfredo replied. "The odds are up ten to one," he coughed. "Don't waste your money."

"You hear that little traitor of the great Ted Williams," Mario said. "Oh ye of little faith. How 'bout you, Pat?"

"Gee, I don't know. He's pretty used up. The man's forty-two for God's sake," Pat said. "Anyway, you cleaned me out."

"Don't look at me," Carlo said. "He's not Italian, what do I care? Come on, he's an old man."

Mario looked at Eddie with his pleading face.

"What?" Eddie asked. "You want me to bet on a miracle?"

"Yeah," Mario said. "How much you got?"

"Twenty-five bucks," Eddie replied, "but if I go, you go."

Mario counted off twenty-five dollars from his winnings. Eddie added his own and handed it to Alfredo. "Fifty for a homer."

Alfredo sucked his teeth and took the money. "You got it, Eddie," Alfredo said, clearing his throat with a deep rattle. "Last call! Anyone else?" There were no other takers.

"He's stepping in the box," the announcer said. "He's pawing the dirt with his left foot, just like these last twenty-two seasons. It's an amazing moment, fans...Williams is settling into his stance. You can't hear a thing...there's the windup from Fisher...there's the pitch...Ball one." The crowd noise started to grow again.

"Man, this is great," Mario said, standing near the radio with Eddie. The others crowded around.

"Here's the windup for the second pitch," the announcer said with excitement, and "Williams unleashes a mighty cut." The crowd groaned. "But it's a miss."

"Holy crap!" Mario blurted out. "He's the best!"

"He's tired like me," Alfredo said with a grin. "You shouldn't expect too much."

The announcer started up again. "Williams is set...and there's Fisher's next pitch...and Williams swings and he connects!" The noise of the crowd swamped the speaker. "It's back...back...oh my God, it's off the roof of the bullpen! Home run! Home run!"

Mario and Eddie jumped up and down with Pat and Carlo. Alfredo looked on, his face a little worried, his fingers tapping lightly on the cash box.

"Williams is galloping around the bases," the announcer practically wept. "No home run trot for Ted, what a magical moment! The crowd is going wild. A fairy tale ending. There's no tip of the cap, no, and there he goes, head down, into the dugout. Five hundred twenty-one home runs, third all-time homer list behind the Babe and Jimmy Foxx, unbelievable!"

"Oh my God!" Mario said and turned to Alfredo, who counted out the money. "Two-fifty apiece. Enjoy!"

Pat opened the cake box and offered up a two-layered white cake. "It's on the house," he said as he sliced up the cake into thick slices.

"Here's to Ted," they cheered, taking big, sloppy bites.

"The crowd is still roaring for him to come out," the announcer said, "but he won't come out and doff his hat. That's Ted Williams for you."

"Yeah, and it's Ted Williams Day," Mario said. "Paper said the Mayor proclaimed today his day."

"Mayor Cowley?" Carlo asked. "He's been a busy man."

"Cowley was down here yesterday, selling the West End down the river," Eddie said.

"Ted wouldn't like that," Mario replied.

"Listen, I gotta go," Eddie said. "I got some shopping to do. I'll see you fellas later. Drop in on my daughter's birthday party tonight. You're all invited."

A chorus of thank yous and congratulations rang around the room.

"I'll see you tonight, Mario. Thanks for strong-arming me on the bet."

"Hey Eddie," Mario called, pulling at Eddie's sleeve.

"What?"

"Ted Williams, he's one helluva guy, ain't he?"

"Right he is. He's taken some cheap shots from the papers. But he's like us, he doesn't give up."

"Yeah," replied Mario, nodding his head in agreement.

Eddie smiled as he made his way to the door. "Take care now," Eddie said. "'Til tonight. Save some room for some more cake!"

3

THE PARTY

Eddie left The Club and squinted in the milky light of the overcast day. He walked along a narrow, curving street lined with tenements. Near the corner he passed several small cafes, fruit stands, and meat markets. He once again felt the pride he had for the West End. The old-timers said it still kept the memory of the southern cities of Italia. The sidewalks were crowded with older Italian immigrants, first-generation people, whom he knew by name; they liked to sit on the tenement steps or on their favorite chairs out front. Kids played stick ball down a side street and teens released from school congregated on the corners. He spotted a group of young males slick fighting, faking their punches, roughing each other up, laughing and swaying on the curb.

Eddie glanced in a drug store window and paused to check out his haircut again. He smiled at Mr. Costa waving from behind the counter inside. As he walked on with a rolling, self-confident stride, Eddie passed Joe Renaldo's fruit stand, and Joe, who had a pencil tucked behind an ear, tossed him an orange from a new crate.

"Hey, lookin' good, Eddie," he shouted. "Where you goin'? Got a date?"

"Yeah, well maybe," Eddie said. "With two real cute gals."

"Oh, yeah," Joe laughed. "I saw them around here. I think one's about to have a birthday, eh?"

"You got it...and I've got a little shopping to do."

Eddie walked down to the main thoroughfare on Beckett Street and stepped into Guys and Dolls Toy Shop. The front was filled with dozens of dolls.

For a few moments, Eddie was confused. There were so many to pick from, but after looking at baby dolls and Barbie dolls, Eddie found the one for his Catharine. It had a frilly pink dress, thick petticoats, white tights, and dark hair in pony tails with pink ribbons on the end. The doll's pert face actually reminded him a little of his daughter's.

On the games rack, he picked out a wooden puzzle with big pieces; she'd need that in a few more months. God, she was growing so quickly, learning new things every day. The puzzle showed a little girl wearing a yellow raincoat chasing after a fat white duck, both splashing through a big blue puddle.

Eddie paid for the toys, walked back into the West End and dropped into Pat's Italian Bakery. The glass counters held cream puffs, cannolis, sugar cookies, cinnamon breads, colorful amaretto cakes and cookies, and brownies. Pat came out of the back.

"Hey Pat, you got my cake ready?" Eddie asked.

"You bet. The perfect cake for Catharine's first birthday."

Pat brought out a large white box from the refrigerator and slid it across the counter. Eddie opened the lid and took a peek—a white cake with hearts and flowers, and in the center a miniature baby doll.

"My best," Pat said.

"It's a work of art, thanks."

"It has three layers, all soaked with rum," Pat exclaimed, kissing his fingertips.

Eddie pointed to the baby doll. "Whose idea was that?"

"What am I? A dentist, or a baker? The baby can play with it."

"It's great, Pat. What do I owe you?"

"Forget it. Get outta here. It's my gift to Catharine."

Eddie knew not to argue. "Thanks Pat. You're coming by, I hope?"

"I wouldn't miss it for the world. I'll be by about seven, after I close the shop."

Eddie walked down the street to his tenement building, the old red brick, three–decker he'd known since childhood. He balanced the cake and climbed the stairs to the foyer. The peeling plaster hallways echoed with babies crying, Italian music, and a medley of voices in English and Italian. Two of the small boys in the tenement, Nunzio and Billy, were bouncing a ragged tennis ball off the wall above the radiator. Nunzio, Eddie's-five-year old nephew, had an impish face and bright black eyes; he ran forward and sniffed at the box.

"Cake, definitely, cake," he said. His nose quivered.

"Good sniffer you got there," Eddie remarked as he gave Nunzio a look. "You and Billy coming up tonight for Catharine's party?"

"Sure," Nunzio answered, "and Mom's already got a present, but she won't tell me what it is, she thinks I'll squeal."

"Naw, you wouldn't squeal."

"Would too," Billy chimed in from across the foyer.

"He's a jerk," Nunzio said. "What does he know? He's a year ahead in school, that's all."

"Yeah, what's the big deal?" Eddie asked. "I know you can keep a secret."

Nunzio nodded his head and dashed back to his ball game.

Eddie climbed with steady steps to the top landing on the third floor and opened the door to his apartment. He heard Anna singing in the kitchen.

Eddie paused in the hallway and watched Anna, her back to him. She had long, silky black hair that glistened in the light, and her dark olive skin made her a classic Italian beauty, striking in an old country kind of way. He had known her since childhood. She grew up on the neighboring street. In June, she had turned twenty and he couldn't believe she was so grown up, a mother, his wife.

After she and Eddie had married last year, Anna's parents and younger brother and sister moved into the vacant apartment on the second floor. Eddie's mother had died two years before his marriage; she was a victim of a single, massive stroke. The doctors said there was no pain, just a door opening to a higher spiritual existence.

Eddie stayed on in his mother's place on the third floor. Now, with Anna in the apartment, the old place had a mixed look, old country first generation, his mother's second generation, and now Anna's newer, third generation American look.

In the living room were a vinyl couch and a shiny, inexpensive coffee table he and Anna had purchased. In the dining room was an imitation mahogany dining room set. On the wall hung several ceramic Madonnas that had once belonged to his Grandmother. Mixed in were old photos from the early years in the West End; some copper-tinted plates were brought from Italy by his grandparents. There were many happy memories here.

Anna turned. "Oh, I didn't hear you," she said.

Eddie smiled and dropped his packages on the kitchen table. Then he put his arms around his lovely wife and kissed her warm lips. "Uhmmm, that's good," he said.

"So how did it go this morning?" Anna asked as she looked at his bag of presents and the cake box.

"Oh these," Eddie waved at the gifts. "Good, And, hey, I had a fine stroke of luck with Mario over at The Club."

"Hmmm...sometimes I don't know about that Mario. You two take off work early; I hope you made a little money."

Eddie felt a surge of anger. "Hey, don't worry. I picked up a little change," he said, "and we cleared the day off with the boss at work. I told you that already."

"I just worry about you getting a reputation, you know, for goofing off like Mario."

"What? It's my daughter's first birthday. Can't a guy get off early?"

"Sure, but I can tell you don't like this job either," Anna said. "I was planning on studying accounting at the community college before I got pregnant."

"Come on, honey, don't start that again," Eddie said, backing up.

Anna shrugged and smiled. "Wouldn't it be fun if we both went to school together? You could study business management. We'd form a team and start our own business. I've been thinking about that lately," Anna admitted.

"Whoa! Not so fast! Let's get our kid grown up a little more, then we'll see, huh?" Eddie looked around the kitchen. "Say, where is the bambina?"

"Sleeping," Anna replied, pointing at the white box on the kitchen table. "Is that the cake?"

"Wait 'til you see it. Pat did a beautiful job. And here're a couple of nice things for her." He pulled them out of the bag.

Anna laughed. "She's too young for a puzzle, Eddie, but I guess she'll enjoy chewing the wood blocks. This doll is beautiful."

"You really think she's too young?" Eddie questioned Anna. "She's a Sveglio, she'll have a mechanical ability. You wait and see...You really think I did bad?"

"No, come on, you did good," Anna said. "Catharine will love all these things."

There was a light knock at the kitchen door and Anna's mother, Rosa, entered. She had a dark complexion like Anna, and her quick, mischievous smile always made Eddie like her.

"Hi, I'm here to do the salad," Rosa said as she kissed Eddie on the cheek. "Hello, Eddie, sweetheart, I'm so glad you got the day off."

"Ma," Anna said. "I've just been sayin' the opposite."

"See," Eddie said.

"He works too hard, Anna," Rosa said, kissing him again. "What do you expect here, a saint? Oh, the cake, let's see."

Eddie pulled down the sides of the box and showed off the birthday cake.

"Ahhh , *preciosa!*" Anna and her mother sighed together.

By half past seven, Eddie worked his way through the standing-room-only crowd in his kitchen. "Coming through, coming through, excuse me," he said.

He reached the kitchen table holding the lighter he brought from the coffee table in the living room. He snapped the lighter twice before a third caught. Catharine's eyes widened in surprise.

Eddie lit the two candles on the cake. "One for one and one to grow on," Anna said.

Eddie looked around. All eyes were on the baby. Catharine sat in her high chair and stared at the cake. The two candles burned in front of the pink doll baby.

"Make a wish," Anna said to Catharine.

"Arghhh...mama." Catharine stretched out her arms toward Anna.

"Don't forget your daddy," Eddie said, kissing his daughter.

"Come on, blow!" Eddie puckered his lips and blew for Catharine. Nunzio appeared from under the table and added his hot breath. The candle's flame swelled, burned away from the wick, and went out. A trail of gray smoke rose above the cake.

Salvatore, a neighbor from next door, squeezed his accordion, and broke into "Happy Birthday." The roomful of people, old and young alike, joined in. When they finished, everyone applauded. Anna cut the cake and served the first piece to Catharine, who poked her fingers into the frosting and then into in her mouth. She smiled with joy.

Eddie served the second piece to Mr. Lazzaro. A first generation immigrant, Mr. Lazzaro owned the building and had become a surrogate grandfather to its many tenants. Eddie wanted him to feel important, remembered, and honored.

Mr. Lazzaro had attended all his parties and the most important events in his life. He had helped his mother after his father died in Europe.

Tonight, as usual, Mr. Lazzaro was dressed in an old, navy blue pinstriped suit. His face was calm with authority and sympathy. He pushed back his chair and stood up. The room fell silent. He held up a glass of red wine. "Let us toast Catharine on her first birthday. May God grant her good health and a long happy life. God bless her and her parents."

Everyone raised their glasses and cheered in unison, "*Saluta!*"

"Thank you, Mr. Lazzaro," Eddie said to him. "That was nice."

Salvatore played the accordion again. A young couple from the first floor, Tony and wife, Jenny Moretta, who was Angelino's cousin, danced in the living room, while Catharine clapped puzzle pieces in time to the music. The baby doll from atop the cake lay on the tray with icing on its feet and head.

Anna kissed Catharine and spotted part of a pink icing rose stuck in her own long hair. "Oh, you're sweet as sugar," Anna said, kissing the baby again.

Nunzio danced with his older sister Louise, who towered over him. Sitting at one end of the table watching the couples dancing were Anna's mother, sister and brother, Salvatore's wife Rosa, and Aunt Lucy. Eddie, Mario and his father Paolo, Pat the baker, and Anna's father Casimo, all sat at the other end of the table talking and smoking stogies.

After the dancing had stopped for a few moments, Anna came over to Eddie and whispered in his ear. "Why don't you ask Mr. Lazzaro to sing?"

Eddie nodded yes and went over to Mr. Lazzaro, who was making a fuss over Catharine. "How about singing for us?"

Mr. Lazzaro whispered, "Who wants to hear an old man sing? I don't have the voice I once had."

"What do you mean? You're as good as Caruso," Eddie said. "Come on, Mr. Lazzaro. We love hearing you sing. Hey, don't I hear you always singing from across the landing?"

"*Sí*, and that should be enough torture, eh? But, okay, what should I sing?"

"How about Core 'Ngrato?" Anna suggested.

"For the baby and for my wife," Mr. Lazzaro said. "I wish Catharine could be here to see her namesake reach the grand old age of one. She always loved parties."

"I know she did," Eddie agreed, patting the old man on the arm. "It's okay, she'd want you to sing."

"With that, how can I say no?"

Eddie called to Angelo and the others. "Our own Caruso is going to sing for us. Come on, everybody."

Everyone gathered around the baby and she looked up at Mr. Lazzaro. His hand rested on her arm as he began singing the old melancholy melody. His voice was vibrant and tender, if not quite professional. The feeling was enough to bring tears to the eyes of most in the room. When he finished, everyone applauded, shouting "Bravo! Bravo!"

Anna kissed Catharine and Eddie hugged Mr. Lazzaro.

"Wonderful!" Eddie exclaimed. "See, you still got your voice."

Mr. Lazzaro nodded and squeezed Eddie's arm, and then bent down to kiss Catharine's forehead.

4

THE FISH SELLER

Mr. Lazzaro awoke at 6:00 AM on Saturday morning, an hour earlier than his usual routine. He felt uneasy, nervous about something. His stomach was in knots and his head ached. Maybe it was the party and perhaps a little too much wine. Lately he had been feeling tired, and there were moments when he had to lie down and put his feet up. He shuffled into the bathroom and moistened his hair brush with a dab of bay rum. He stroked his hair and barely touched the white strands with the bristles, and then the tea kettle began to whistle in the kitchen.

He looked in the mirror again. "That's fine," he said. He walked out to the kitchen, poured hot water in a cup, dipped his tea bag, and went out again into the parlor. He eased down in his rocker and sipped the tea. The parlor was first generation style, with an overstuffed couch, comfortable chairs, and an antique grandfather clock. On the flowered wallpaper hung sculptured crucifixes, an art print of Christ and the Madonna, and a Botticelli print of a Venus from the sea. Dusty lace doilies rested on the table and bureau tops.

Mr. Lazzaro stared at a photograph of his deceased wife, Catharine. The silver frame was draped in black. He put down his tea, closed his eyes, and rocked back and forth.

He was in the kitchen. Catherine was taking eggs from the refrigerator. She filled a glass half full of wine, turned, and called to him in Italian.

"How many eggs Joseph? One or two?" she asked, smiling.

"Two," he answered, stepping into the kitchen from the bedroom.

Catharine broke the eggs into the wine. He pulled his suspenders up over his shoulders.

"It's on the table," she said.

"Thank you," said Mr. Lazzaro.

Catharine sliced a loaf of crusty bread while Mr. Lazzaro gulped down the egg and wine mixture. He smacked his lips.

"Ahh, the wine is getting better," he said. Then he sang. "Fi-ga-ro! Fi-ga-ro!"

"You're in good form," Catharine said. "Sit down now."

On the table were the sliced bread, coffee, and a bowl of fresh fruit. Mr. Lazzaro dunked the bread into the fresh perked coffee.

"Some fruit?" Catharine offered.

"A pomegranate."

She handed him the ruby-red fruit.

"You're feeling good today," she said.

"I've never felt better." He laughed and saw her face dissolve into mist. "Catharine? Catharine?"

The grandfather clock chimed and Mr. Lazzaro tried to see her face, but it blurred.

He jerked forward in the rocker, his eyes stared ahead, and the silence brought him back to the present, alone again. His heart pounded an odd rhythm. He stared at the grandfather clock which indicated it was seven o'clock. Realizing it was time to go to work, he rose to his feet.

Mr. Lazzaro left the tenement and walked six blocks through the commercial warehouse district, arriving at the fish piers on Boston Harbor. He pulled a tarp off his green vendor's cart and pushed it up the main dock.

His lifelong friend, Luigi Bono, was unloading the day's catch from his boat, *The Mermaid*. Luigi was a wiry seventy-year-old with a gray scraggly beard and a leathery face.

"*Buon giorno*, Joseph," Luigi said. Sun wrinkles flashed around his eyes.

"*Buon giorno*, Luigi. What's the catch today?"

"Haddock, cod, just about everything. I even have calamari."

"Let me have about twenty pounds of each," Mr. Lazzaro said, rolling his cart next to the gangplank. Luigi helped him load the cart with fish.

"So, Joseph, how was the baby's party?" Luigi inquired.

"Oh, my friend, a true fiesta, you missed some good fettuccine. And oh, my homemade wine," Mr. Lazzaro said.

"I'm so sorry, but the fish were really biting last night, and the sunset, it was so beautiful," Luigi said. "Reminded me of Sicily, the old fishing days with my brothers."

Mr. Lazzaro nodded his head in understanding. "I miss Italia now more than ever, especially lately. It's strange. I'm feeling this..." Mr. Lazzaro sighed and arranged the last fish on the top. Together they began to pack the fish down in ice.

"You know, I still have more wine in the cellar," Mr. Lazzaro said. "Why don't you come over tonight and try a glass, for old time's sake?"

Luigi eyed his old friend. "Good, I'll be seeing you tonight."

"Tonight then. Ciao."

Mr. Lazzaro pushed the heavy cart toward the street market area for the West End. Rows of carts and stands heaped with fresh fruit and vegetables filled the area.

"Hey, we got fresh lemons over here from Florida," one man said to the shoppers with their bags.

"Apples, we got apples from all over New England. Take a look, ladies," another barker said, pointing at his pyramids of the fall harvest.

"Hey, Mr. Lazzaro," another man shouted. "Fine day, eh?"

Mr. Lazzaro nodded to all and rolled his cart on to his favorite, northeast corner. He parked his cart and greeted his first customer of the day, Mrs. Calvi. One of his oldest customers, Mrs. Calvi, gray-haired, and hump-backed, pulled her small grocery cart toward him. She conducted her standard inspection of his offerings.

"Ahh, you've got calamari this Saturday," Mrs. Calvi said in her high-pitched voice. "So, Luigi had a good catch last night? I'll have a half dozen. I hope they're fresh, Mr. Lazzaro."

"Fresh today, Mrs. Calvi," he said, tossing the squid on the scale. "And how are you doing?"

"Oh, you know, good as can be. And how much will that cost?"

"Two dollars even."

"*Ma-ma-mea*! Too expensive!"

"Okay, okay, a dollar seventy-five. How's that?"

"That's much better." Mrs. Calvi smiled and counted out the money from her coin purse. Mr. Lazzaro handed her the package and she arranged it in her shopping bag.

"Ciao, 'til next time," she said with a hint of a triumphant smile.

"Ciao, Mrs. Calvi," Mr. Lazzaro responded.

Mr. Lazzaro looked past her and saw Eddie enter the market-place. He waved at him.

"Good morning," Eddie looked in the cart. "Hey, you got a great selection today."

"Not bad. Luigi had a good run," Mr. Lazzaro explained.

"All the better for you, huh?"

"Yeah, I'm doing okay, and you?" Mr. Lazzaro asked.

Eddie shrugged. "You know, up and down. The work right now isn't much. That same warehouse job Mario snagged."

"Don't worry. You got your Anna and Catharine, that's better than any job. That was a nice party last night. Little Catharine is so sweet."

"Yes, she had a good time, we all did. By the way, you sounded like a great opera singer."

"*Grazie, grazie,*" Mr. Lazzaro said, rearranging a cod fish.

"Well, I'll see you later. I'm just out runnin' a few errands."

"Wait," Mr. Lazzaro said. "Take some fresh calamari to Anna. Have a nice dinner, on me. Come on."

"Calamari? Well, I wasn't headed right back, but okay...you're spoiling us again."

"And what's so bad about that, eh?" Mr. Lazzaro winked at Eddie.

"Hey, you get some rest this weekend," Eddie said. "You're lookin' tired."

"You too, young man," Mr. Lazzaro reciprocated. "Once in awhile you need to sleep late and hang out on the steps. No need to rush."

Eddie felt a wave of release, thinking about the happy hours he had spent during his childhood, many hanging out with family and neighbors on the tenement streets. He pointed his finger at Mr. Lazzaro. "You know, sometimes you old guys come up with some good ideas. It's a miracle."

"Hey, you wise guy," said Mr. Lazzaro. "Now get outta here. Take the calamari. Take a day off. Enjoy it."

5

EDDIE AND ANNA

*M*onday *morning Eddie boarded the crowded Green Line trolley for* work. The cars were packed, standing room only. He rocked along and glanced over a businessman's shoulder at the sports page. The writers were squeezing mileage out of Ted Williams's final at bat. "What a magnificent home run, what a way to end a career. Eddie thought to himself. *But why didn't he come out to acknowledge the cheers of the fans? Maybe false modesty, maybe he was sick of the press. Still, he was a classic New Englander, flinty hard, unrelenting.*

The trolley clattered north across the Charles River and skirted the harbor works. Eddie stepped off onto the platform in East Cambridge and breathed in the cool early morning air, a contrast to the stale air of the cramped ride. Down the street, workers filed through the factory gate of the huge assembly and distribution firm, System Tech. Eddie joined them. He walked by the timekeeper and security booths and punched the time clock. Mario waited for him.

"How'd your weekend go?" Eddie asked.

"Fine, 'til I read the papers," said Mario.

"What?"

"About the West End," Mario clarified. "Did you see Angel in the picture with the Mayor and his gang?"

"I talked to him," Eddie said.

"Jesus, what a jackass." Did you tell him to..."

"Take a hike?" Eddie interjected. "Yeah, well, just about. There was a lot of brass around. Can you believe the nerve of that guy? Man, it's like people will sell out for nothin'. Send a kid to Harvard on a full scholarship, and look at the weasel you get back."

"I'm glad I never bothered with college. It does something to you," Mario said as he studied Eddie. "You almost went, didn't you?"

"Hey, I still might, but I won't do that to my people. Never."

"Holy cow! Here's another weasel," Mario said, nodding toward the foreman headed their way. "It's Bill Clipboard."

"Hey, you two, you take a day off like you're important business tycoons," Bill said, glancing at his clipboard. "So, I've got a special job for you two. Come on."

Bill marched down the dock and led them to the entrance of a battleship-gray warehouse, its contents sealed behind aircraft hangar steel doors. He pushed a button on the wall and the doors slid open on rails the size of train tracks. Inside the cavernous depths, Eddie and Mario saw rows of boxes stacked with circuit board panels.

"Okay, wise guys, here's a little project that should keep you busy for a couple of hours," the foreman said. "Watch closely..." He picked up a panel, marked it with a rubber stamp, and placed it in a padded shipping box. "Now that wasn't so bad, was it? Any questions?"

Eddie looked at the panels and frowned.

"Well," the foreman said. "What are you waiting for, a personal introduction?"

"Hey, Bill, thanks, this is just my kind of job," Mario laughed and nudged Eddie. "Come on, this represents job security."

Bill lit up a cigarette and walked off. "I'll be back later," he said. "No messing around."

Eddie started to say something, but Mario tugged his arm.

"Let it go, he's a jerk," Mario said.

"Yeah, come on, let's get busy." Eddie started wading through the boxes of panels. "Looks like six months of work here."

That same morning, like she did every Monday morning, Anna took Catharine along shopping at Cohen's Deli in the West End. She bought a pound of provolone and pastrami and paid Josh Cohen, the owner's son. Today Josh was sporting a new mustache.

31

"What do you think?" Josh asked, pointing to his new mustache. Anna smiled and laughed.

"Ah, come on," Josh said. "It's not that bad!"

"No, I think it's fine." Anna couldn't stop smiling. "It's just you look like you could be a Mexican *bandido*...like in the movies."

"A Jewish Zapata—a revolutionary, now, that I like," Josh admitted and grinned from ear to ear. "*Gracias.*"

Anna laughed and kissed Catharine.

"She's a doll," Josh said, smiling at Anna. "Say, how's Eddie?"

"He's doing fine," she answered. "Mario got him a job at System Tech."

"Oh, the computer people in Cambridge. That's good. There's a future in computers, people say."

"Well, maybe," Anna said. She smiled and tucked her groceries in her shopping bag. "We'll see you later, Josh."

"Okay, Anna, take care. Bye bye, sweetheart," Josh said as he waved back at Catharine's farewell.

Anna stepped out on the street and saw a crowd of local residents gathered on the corner. "Come on, Catharine. Let's see what's going on."

"I'm just here to map the area," said a middle-aged man in construction clothes. At his feet lay a tripod and surveying poles. Mrs. Petrini, a widow in her sixties who owned the flower shop nearby was the first to speak up.

"And what is this all for?" Mrs. Petrini asked as she pointed at the equipment. "You're not coming through my store, no sir."

"Don't you people read the papers?" the surveyor's young assistant asked. The City is going to redevelop this area."

"Redevelop? It's fine the way it is," Mrs. Petrini snapped back.

"Hey, we're just doing our job for the City of Boston," the older surveyor said.

Mr. Donatello, a sixty-year West End resident, cleared his throat and said, "Hear us and hear us good. You go back and tell your boss we don't want no redevelopment around here. You got it?"

"Come on, that's enough excitement," Mrs. Petrini said. "Let's break this up."

Anna walked away with Catharine and stopped across the street to see what was going to happen. The surveyors saw the locals watching them. They didn't delay for long. They picked up their equipment and loaded it into a nearby City truck and drove away, leaving a cloud of blue exhaust smoke behind.

"Good riddance," someone yelled out from a window overlooking the street.

Catharine whimpered and began to cry. Anna carried her back to her baby carriage parked outside Cohen's Deli and tucked her inside. "Everything's gonna be fine, sweetie," Anna said, even though she couldn't muster up a smile. "Don't you worry."

Eddie and Mario washed up in the factory locker room. The door opened and Bill swaggered in.

"Hi Boss, you're lookin' cool," Mario said and smiled. "Got a hot date after work?"

"I don't know about you, Mario," Bill said as he stepped between Mario and Eddie before the row of mirrors. "You're too much of a joker."

"What's with you, pal?" Eddie asked. "What's your gripe?"

"Yeah, we love it here," Mario said.

"You guys haven't been the best," the foreman said, staring at them in the mirror. "But I better not catch you guys lying down on the job...if you catch my drift. There's plenty of guys lookin' for work. You know what I mean?"

"Hey, what's this?" Mario stepped between Eddie and Bill. "Now, now, Boss, you know we love our work."

Overhead the loudspeaker paged, "Bill Lakers, please pick up, Bill Lakers." Bill shook a twisted forefinger in warning and walked away.

"Jesus, what a jerk," Mario said, winking at Eddie. "Come on. Let's get outta here before he thinks of something else to gripe about."

"Mario, I don't know if this is going to work out," Eddie said. He tucked his comb in his back pocket. "I mean, I appreciate you getting me on here, but I don't know."

"Hey, don't worry, the shift's over. We did good work. The guy's a complete moron."

Eddie and Mario left the plant and strolled past the stores on the street to the Green Line station. They came to a department store window decorated with female mannequins decked out in sexy nightgowns.

"Whoa, this is some window," Mario said after giving a loud whistle. He looked at himself in the plate glass and checked out his wavy hair and bright white smile. "Hey, and look at the handsome guys taking a close look at the peep show!"

"Boy," Eddie said. "I bet Anna would look real nice in that. Let's check it out."

They went in through the revolving doors and found the women's lingerie department. A young blonde woman with thick makeup and heavy perfume came over to them. "May I help you?" she asked in a husky voice.

"How much are the negligees in the window out front?"

"Oh," she said smiling. "Those are very popular. They're on sale, only twenty dollars."

"I'd like to see the different color choices," Eddie said.

"Certainly, I'll get them for you." She swung her hips as she stepped behind the counter. "They come in red, black, white, and blue."

Mario whistled and fluttered his hand in appreciation. "I think I'm in love," he whispered to Eddie.

"Yeah, sure," Eddie said.

"Beg your pardon," the woman said, laying the negligees on the glass counter. "What size does your girlfriend wear?"

"Well, it's for my wife. She's a little shorter than you, maybe a little..." Eddie widened the space between his hands. "Heavier?"

"Fuller, we women prefer that term," she said and smiled.

"Well, it's hard for me to tell exactly," Eddie said.

The woman stood up to her full height. She picked up the black negligee and held it up against herself.

"I think Anna has a little bit more in here," Mario said, pointing to the woman's bosom. "Yeah, a little less in the waist, but much more here." Mario started to pat the woman's hip, but she stepped back.

Eddie frowned at Mario and shook his head.

"Please," the saleswoman said to Mario and turned to Eddie. "She may wear an eleven, that's what size this is. If it doesn't fit, she can always return it."

"I'll take it," Eddie responded. "But give me the white one. And can you put it in a nice box?"

"Certainly, just a moment," the saleswoman said, taking the white negligee to the back of the store.

"While you wait, I'm gonna look around," Mario said, pointing toward the men's clothing section.

The saleswoman returned and Eddie paid her. He took his wrapped gift and searched the men's department for Mario. He found him pawing through the discounted silk tie rack.

"Ah, they got nothing here," Mario complained. "I'll look like a carnival barker. I wanna look like somebody in show biz, you know, a producer or something."

"Later, Mr. DeMille, let's get moving," Eddie said. "We've got a train to catch."

They headed for the revolving doors to the street. Mario grabbed Eddie and stopped him. He pointed to a male mannequin sporting only a T-shirt and undershorts. "Hey, Eddie, look at that poor guy. Poor fool, he's missing something."

"What are you talking about?" Eddie asked.

Mario picked up a T-shirt from the counter and rolled it into a cylinder. He glanced up and down the aisles and then suddenly stuffed the tube into the mannequin's undershorts.

"Jesus," Eddie blurted out. "You're crazy, you know that."

Mario pulled Eddie behind a suit rack and made him watch. Two ladies in their fifties strolled by and halted. One gasped and the other giggled. Eddie gave Mario a yank and shoved him through the revolving doors. Outside he hustled him toward the subway.

"Was that great or what?" Mario exclaimed.

"You oughta be certified," Eddie said, pushing him onto the Green Line for the West End.

Eddie slipped into his apartment and tiptoed into the kitchen. Anna had her back to him and was stirring a pot on the stove. Catharine sat in her high chair, banging a wooden spoon. Eddie held the box behind his back and bent down to kiss Catharine.

"Da-da," she said with a squeal, causing Anna to turn around.

"Oh, you scared me! What's Daddy up to now?" she said.

"I've got a surprise for you. Now close your eyes." Eddie motioned for her to turn toward the window over the sink. Through the window he could see another row of tenements and a piece of late afternoon sky.

Anna's long black hair reached the middle of her back, even when it was tied in a loose bow. He reached out and stroked it. Eddie gave her a kiss on the back of her head and laid the box on the table.

"Okay, turn around," he said.

"Ohhh, why Eddie. What did you do? Another present for Catharine?" Anna winked at the baby.

"No," Eddie replied. "Catharine was Friday. Today's your day." Catharine slapped at a bowl of pudding with a curled silver spoon and said, "Da-da, ma-ma, da-da-ma-ma."

Anna struggled with the tape on the box. "I wonder what Daddy has been up to? Hmmm..."

Eddie reached over and snapped open the box.

"Now, be patient, Daddy," Anna said. She pulled back the lid and the blue tissue paper. "Ohhh, my goodness, what is this?" She lifted the negligee from the box and held it in front of Catharine and Eddie. Catharine's tiny fingers reached for it.

"Ohhh, how beautiful!" Anna exclaimed. "Catharine, this is definitely not for you, huh?"

She gave Eddie a wet kiss on the lips and held the negligee against her front. "This is very pretty, Eddie, but can we afford this?"

"Sure," Eddie said. "Ted Williams paid for it."

"What?"

"Just kidding. Come on," he said jokingly. "Try it on. I bet you look like a movie star."

"Oh, that's my competition, huh?" Anna asked. "Well, I'll try it on after Catharine goes to bed, which should be very soon. See the way she's rubbing her ears with her pudding spoon."

"Yeah, I see that all too well," Eddie said as he took the spoon from Catharine. "Hey, you don't want pudding in your ears, silly."

Eddie helped Anna clean up Catharine and then they put her down in her crib.

Anna led Eddie to the living room.

"You wait here while I try it on," she instructed.

"Sure," Eddie said as he sat on the couch. He glanced at the papers and caught sight of another article about the West End and redevelopment.

"I feel like I'm not wearing anything," Anna called out from the bedroom.

"Great, that's the idea," Eddie said turning the paper over. "Can I come in now? Let me see."

"Okay, I'm ready, I think," Anna announced. The door opened slightly. Her hand fluttered in the soft light of the darkened bedroom and waved him in.

"Oh man," Eddie said, as he sprang for the bedroom. She lay down across the bed. He went to his wife and kissed her. She had added a dab of perfume and he kissed her neck and shoulder. Soon his hands and lips were all over her body, and she began undressing him. He tried to take the negligee off over her head, but it got caught under her hips. She whispered, "Slow down, you'll rip it."

"I don't care," he said. "I'll get another one." But she sat up against him and pressed her breasts against his chest and he slipped the thin nightie off. He tossed it through the air to the bedroom floor.

"Anna...Anna, I love you," Eddie said. A moment later he gasped as he entered her and rocked her under his hips.

"Oh Eddie," she said gasping herself. "Don't stop...don't stop, honey."

Eddie and Ann rested in each other's arms.

"Look at that sky," Eddie said. "It's beautiful."

Anna sat up. "Oh, I almost forgot. I've invited Mr. Lazzaro for dinner!" she remembered. She sprang up and started dressing. "I need to tell you about something that happened today."

"Okay," Eddie said after having groaned. "But let's have a glass of wine while we talk it over."

In the kitchen Anna chopped onions for dinner and Eddie poured two glasses of Mr. Lazzaro's chilled wine from the birthday party. Anna told him about the incident with the surveyors. Eddie listened with a gloomy expression on his face.

"I know you think of Mr. Lazzaro like a father, we all do," Anna said. "It worries me. What if they take his building? What will that do to him? Where will we all go?"

"Anna, look, don't worry for now," Eddie tried to comfort her. "Maybe it's just a lot of publicity. I'll look into it, okay?"

A knock came at the front door.

"That must be Mr. Lazzaro," Anna said. "Let him in, won't you?"

"Let's not go into this stuff, unless he brings it up," Eddie suggested. "I don't want to worry him, you know, so let's have a nice quiet meal."

He went into the hallway to let in his old friend. Since his earliest days, when Eddie and his mother would eat dinner alone, he had the fondest memories of Mr. Lazzaro. He was always welcome to drop in for dinners and make the table complete with his stories of the old country, as well as the current gossip, trivial and substantial, in the West End and beyond. Eddie was pleased Anna had taken to Mr. Lazzaro. Maybe it was because Mr. Lazzaro was like a doting grandfather to little Catharine. How good it felt having Mr. Lazzaro now in Catherine's life. He wanted her childhood to be filled with memories like his own, of Mr. Lazzaro and the tenement.

6

LETTERS

Eddie and Mario met to drink beer at The Club's bar. The evening news was on TV.

"Last Friday the Federal Government gave the City final approval for the redevelopment of the West End," a reporter said.

Eddie shushed Mario and the others. "Hey Tony. Turn up the TV."

The reporter continued, "Tony Collins spoke with the mayor today. Here is that interview."

Mayor Cowley appeared behind his desk in City Hall. In front of him was the model he had hauled out to the West End on Saturday morning. People in the bar started booing and hissing.

"Who wants to listen to him?" Mario asked. "What a crook!"

Somebody yelled, "He bought City Hall. He doesn't work, just sits on his butt and gives orders."

"Sshhh," Eddie ordered.

The Mayor smiled proudly as the camera zoomed in on the model's high-rise buildings. "The Federal Government has given us one hundred and twenty million dollars for the West End's redevelopment. Now we have the financial support to redevelop one of Boston's most deteriorated neighborhoods."

"How long do you think the redevelopment process will take, Mr. Mayor?" the reporter asked.

"Our developer, Bill O'Mally, estimates it will take no more than three years from start to finish."

Another man in the back of the bar yelled, "Turn that noise off!"

"Do you think they mean it this time?" Eddie asked Mario.

"Nah, they've said this many times before. Something always hangs up the money or something. Besides, knowing the Mayor, if he got that kind of money, he'd spend it on a trip to the Caribbean."

Eddie shook his head sadly. "I hope you're right. I don't need this trouble right now."

"Hey, I wouldn't lose any sleep over it," Mario laughed. "Those micks have never pulled off anything that big."

The next afternoon at work, Eddie and Mario continued to number, sort, and stack the circuit panels for the computers.

"You know, I've been here six months and I still don't know what these things really do," Mario said.

"They use them in computers. They're part of the memory banks that store the information. This is gonna be big business here in Massachusetts. Lots of money in this racket," Eddie said.

"Is that right?" Mario asked, turning one of the panels over. "Well, you could've fooled me. Hey, let's see who can set the fastest pace, okay?"

In a sudden frenzy, they began to pile the parts faster and faster into their compartments, slapping numbers on the outside panel grids. Mario got behind when he dropped a batch on the floor and started flinging parts around the room. Pieces sailed through the air and were pitched into open boxes randomly. One piece hit a support beam and bounced through the open doorway just as the foreman entered. His face was red, a clear indication that he was enraged.

"What is going on!" he shouted. "I want to see you both in my office after this shift."

He started out and then turned back. "Now pick up the mess and get back to work. You guys have been nothing but trouble since you started here. Move it!"

Eddie and Mario left the factory gates without a backward glance.

"It could have been worse," Mario said as he tried to keep up with Eddie's lengthy stride.

"Who you kidding? That was his way of firing us."

"Nah, he just laid us off," Mario tried to convince himself. "Who cares about that stupid job anyway?"

"I do," Eddie said.

"We'll find something else. You don't want to die on a job. Six months is long enough for one haul."

"Yeah, but I've got to find something right away. It's different when you've got a family. I've got to get serious. I need a job. Anna and Catharine depend on me."

"Hey," Mario said, feeling bad about what had happened. "I'll help you find some work. There's always The Club. Buddy can set us up with something."

"That's the solution of last resort," Eddie said.

They took the subway back to the West End and parted at the station. Eddie walked around for a while trying to calm down.

He went up the stairs of the tenement slowly that evening. It was near suppertime. When he came in the door, he was prepared to tell Anna about being fired, but she rushed to him with a frightened look on her lovely face.

"Look at this!" She waved a letter at him.

The envelope said City of Boston on the outside. Eddie quickly scanned the contents.

"When did you get this?"

"It came in this morning's mail. Everybody in the building got one."

"Have you talked with anyone else?"

"I've talked with all the women. Poor Ma, she's so upset. Angelo went into a rage and tore up the letter. Eddie," Anna gasped and sat down on the sofa. "It says we'll be paying our rent to the City of Boston. That means we won't be paying Mr. Lazzaro anymore."

"Have you talked with Mr. Lazzaro?"

"No, I just heard him come home from work a little while ago."

"Maybe I should go talk to him."

"Maybe you should. Your dinner is on the stove. The baby and I have already eaten. You're so late...something wrong?" Anna stared at Eddie.

"Nah, nothing, just had to help Mario with an errand."

"Well, I'm going with the women over to Aunt Lucy's. Maybe she can tell us what will happen."

"Lucy can't forecast the future, it's like the weather. You're asking her to perform a miracle," Eddie said as he refolded the letter.

41

Anna looked at him as if for approval.

"Well, what the heck, I guess it's worth a try, eh?" Eddie said with a sad smile.

Eddie went across the upper landing to Mr. Lazzaro's apartment door. He could hear the singing of Enrico Caruso blaring from a phonograph. After several knocks and no response, Eddie opened the door and peeked in.

"Mr. Lazzaro," he yelled.

Still there was no response. Eddie felt a fear grip him deep inside. Maybe Mr. Lazzaro had fallen or was sick. He entered the apartment, closed the door behind him, and walked toward the parlor, singing out his name. Eddie realized he had repeated this entry so many times down through the years, running errands for his mother or someone else.

Mr. Lazzaro suddenly stepped out from the kitchen.

"Oh Eddie, I thought I heard you. Come in the kitchen. I'm cutting some haddock."

Eddie sat at the table while Mr. Lazzaro gutted the fish at the sink. On the table was the unopened, certified letter from the city.

"Here, let me pour you some wine. I just brought it up from the cellar."

"Just a little," Eddie said. "I haven't had supper yet."

Mr. Lazzaro laughed and, filling Eddie's glass to the brim with the tart red wine, asked, "Will you have supper with me?"

"Thanks," Eddie said, "but Anna has supper waiting for me."

Mr. Lazzaro continued cleaning the fish while Eddie sipped the wine. The Caruso piece was coming to an end and the apartment became momentarily quiet.

"How's your job?"

"Fine, just fine. Would you mind if I turned down the record player?" Eddie asked as he heard another song coming up. "There's something I want to talk to you about."

"Ah, I'm sorry, go ahead."

Eddie went into the parlor and turned it down.

"Isn't Caruso a master?" Mr. Lazzaro said, pausing with a filet dripping over the sink.

"Yup, the best," Eddie agreed.

Mr. Lazzaro cocked his head and smiled at Eddie. "Is there something wrong?"

"Come, sit down."

Mr. Lazzaro took his wine and sat down at the table. Eddie picked up the letter from the table. "It's about this letter from the City."

"Oh...the letter. I planned to have you read it to me. It looks so important."

Eddie opened the envelope and read over it before speaking. "I'm afraid it is important," Eddie said. "Everybody in the building got one. In fact, everybody in the neighborhood got one."

"What does it say?" Mr. Lazzaro asked, his eyebrows knitting together.

"That the city has taken over the neighborhood."

"I don't understand," Mr. Lazzaro said, leaning forward, squinting at the print. "What does this all mean?"

"I'm not sure myself."

"Does it mean they will take away my building?" Mr. Lazzaro asked as he calmly sipped his wine.

"I don't think they can do that. Let's see what happens before we all get upset," Eddie said.

"Who's upset? No letter came in the mail before. Surely there are things we can do...."

"The City is trying to force us to move out."

Mr. Lazzaro nodded his head. "Yes, maybe they're trying to scare the people. Well, this will do it, eh?"

Anna, cradling Catharine in her arms, sat with the other women from the building in Aunt Lucy's parlor around a large round table. Long red peppers hung about the room to ward off evil spirits. The women talked amongst themselves as they awaited Aunt Lucy's entrance.

Jenny, Angel's cousin, a young wife like Anna also from Mr. Lazzaro's building, turned to her and said, "Do you think your aunt can help us?"

"Do you remember when the Rossi boy was so sick?" Anna asked.

"Yes," Jenny answered.

"Even the doctor couldn't find out what was wrong. Lucy visited the boy. Within a few days the boy was up and around."

Anna's mother added, "Even as a young child she had this gift. Once, my grandmother lost her wedding ring. Lucy had a dream. My grandmother found the ring the next morning."

Suddenly, Aunt Lucy, who was in her eighties, appeared through a cloaked doorway, and teetering slightly, made her way cautiously to the table. She sighed and eased down into her seat. Silence engulfed the room. Her silver hair was pulled back tightly in a bun. Her eyes were somewhat unfocused, vacant almost. She was dressed entirely in black, and her pale, white skin seemed to glow with an inner, faint energy.

"It is time to begin now," she said.

She got up slowly and, moving about again carefully, wending her way around the room, she threw salt into all four corners. From a wooden trunk, she pulled out a small silver chest, which she placed upon the table. From the silver chest she removed a lace doily, a sterling silver bowl, and a small silver pitcher.

Before turning off the overhead light, she lit two candles. She started her magic by spreading the doily, filling the bowl with water and the pitcher with olive oil. She then put rosary beads around her neck and stood in a meditative state. Outside, rain was beginning to pound against the windows. The women sat in suspense as she proceeded with the ceremony. Baby Catharine was quieted by the mysterious, tense atmosphere.

Lucy made the sign of the cross, dipped her fingers into the oil, then let a drop of it fall into the water.

"*Malocchio*," Aunt Lucy intensely watched the oil. "It is difficult to see."

"Please," Anna said. She couldn't restrain herself. "Please try."

Aunt Lucy poured another drop of oil into the water and watched closely. Her body swayed. A siren screeched through the streets below. Baby Catharine started to cry.

Aunt Lucy's eyes met those of the women around the table.

"The evil is too big to see," Aunt Lucy said.

"Didn't you see anything?" Jenny asked.

Aunt Lucy spoke firmly, slowly. "It is unclear. It is best sometimes that we do not see. I've seen all I can, but the evil has already been done. It is beyond our grasp."

Aunt Lucy then asked one of the women for a copy of the letter which she took and placed on a metal dish on the table. All watched as she lit a match, then set the letters ablaze. When nothing was left but ash, she arose, walked to the wall, and flipped on the overhead lights. "I think you should go home now."

Eddie was in the parlor watching TV, when he heard Anna in the hall-way fumbling for her keys. He jumped up and opened the door for her.

"Oh, you're back. Good," Anna said. "Listen to that rain."

"Yeah, it's raining like crazy," Eddie said, taking hold of Catharine. "Let me put her to bed. Then we'll talk."

Anna hung up her coat in the closet and went into the baby's room. Eddie, with some difficulty, was undressing Catharine, who was fretting with sleepiness.

When Eddie couldn't get Catharine's undershirt unsnapped, Anna said, "Here, let me do that. Did you talk to Mr. Lazzaro?"

"Yes. He thinks we have a battle on our hands."

"Aunt Lucy wasn't very helpful. After our session she practically pushed us out of her apartment. I've never seen her like that."

"Why?" Eddie said. "What happened?"

"I wish I hadn't gone," Anna said.

"Jesus, what did she say?"

Anna covered Catharine with a soft blanket and gave her a kiss. She was already asleep. Eddie kissed her too and they quickly left the bedroom.

"She said something about the evil being too big. She gave me the jitters. It wasn't so much what she said...it was the way she said it."

Eddie prodded Anna for more details. "What about the way she said it?" Eddie questioned.

Anna replied, "I don't know. I'm tired, exhausted. This has been a hard day."

"Oh come on," Eddie insisted. "I think Aunt Lucy just couldn't get a grip on the situation. It's way out of her league."

"Maybe it's out of our league too," Anna retorted, walking into their bedroom. She began to undress.

Eddie sat on the edge of the bed and watched her as she un-did her hair.

"So, what you're thinking is we should just give in and do what the city tells us," Eddie said, feeling a rush of anger.

"Well, honestly Eddie, at this late date, what choice do we have?" Anna said. "Ma said after the meeting at Aunt Lucy's..."

"What did your mother say?" Eddie snapped.

"Don't be so abrupt," Anna said with a look of disapproval. "She said Dad had been talking about moving to Medford if we don't have a chance. He has a friend at work who has a house for rent. It's big enough for us too."

"For God's sake," Eddie said. "One stinking letter from the City and your Mom and Dad are packing it in!"

"I didn't say that!" Anna rebutted. "They were just talking, that's all."

"Well, believe me, we're not moving. We're gonna fight City Hall and all this nonsense! Mr. Lazzaro said there are things we can do. We're going to do some planning. Maybe form a committee that can do something...Jesus, I grew up here. This is our home and I'm not going to let them take it away without a fight!"

Anna bit her lip and decided to say no more. She sat down on the bed and held Eddie's head against her shoulder. His hands moved slowly down her back, and she felt him beginning to want her. Before long, they were pulling aside the covers and he was kissing her.

7

THE VISIT

The next morning, Eddie and Mario sat in Delma's Coffee Shop. The place was filled with men who stopped for coffee and pastries before going off to work. On the juke box, Frank Sinatra crooned his boast, "I did it my way!"

Mario looked at Eddie and, clearing his throat, tried a new argument. "Look, the boss only laid us off. We'll be able to get back on the day shift in a couple of weeks. Besides, we deserve a vacation."

Eddie turned to Mario. "Gimme a break, Mario. We got the axe. We're canned. Did you tell your old man you were laid off?"

"No. I—," Mario said.

"If you're so sure we were only laid off, why didn't you tell him?"

"I didn't want to trouble him," said Mario.

"Since when did you start to worry about troublin' your old man?" Eddie said and laughed.

"Okay, Sport. Did you tell Anna?"

Eddie frowned. "No, I couldn't. She was all upset over the City's letter. She worries about everything."

Eddie saw Pat the baker carrying in a tray full of freshly baked pastries and bread. He put the tray on the counter.

"Hey, how you doing?" Pat greeted Tony, the burly man behind the counter.

"Could be better. Lot's of trouble brewing around here."

"Yeah, it's always something," Pat said. "Twelve dozen today." He pointed to the tray of pastries and bread.

"Good, it'll be busy," Tony said.

"Give me some coffee will you?" Pat asked.

"Sure," Tony replied.

Pat took the cup and made his way over to Eddie and Mario.

Pat glanced at his watch. "You guys are late today. So, what are you guys, management now?"

"We got canned," Eddie confessed.

"What happened?"

"Short and simple? We were goofing off," Eddie said regretfully.

Mario added, "That foreman had it in for us from the beginning."

"So, what are you going to do now?" Pat asked just before he sipped his coffee.

"I'll try and look for something else. You know, there's some work through The Club," Eddie said, arching his eyebrows.

Pat leaned toward Eddie. "You know if you and Anna need any-thing, you only have to ask. Okay?"

"Thanks, Pat, but I'm all set for now," Eddie reassured him.

Pat gulped down the rest of his coffee and headed out to make more deliveries.

Mario looked at Eddie. "Well, what's on our agenda today, chief?"

"Let's head for The Club. If we stay here, Anna might see me. Then she'll put two and two together. She'll know I lost my job. Then she'll really be worried sick."

"A grown man like you sneaking around corners," Mario re-marked, playfully punching Eddie in the arm. "Come on, it'll all work out. Let's get the morning papers. We'll make some calls, huh?"

"This is on me," Eddie said, tossing down a dollar. "Come on, let's make something happen."

They started out the front door but Mario grabbed Eddie and pointed at a poster on the wall.

"Columbus Day Picnic, Saturday, Holy Name Church. I love that event." Mario sounded like a kid. "And look...Pot Luck dinner, the Roma Band, and my favorite, fireworks. I heard this year they're gon-na do it up right."

"I guess that means you're going?" Eddie said as he pushed Mario through the door.

"No, I'm stayin' home and starin' at the wall!" Mario sarcastically laughed.

"Hey, that might do you some good."

They headed down the street toward The Club. They were within a block of Eddie's home.

"Let's cut through the schoolyard, Mario," Eddie suggested. "I don't want to walk in front of my building. It's got eyes on all three floors."

They walked through the asphalt playground with the kids playing at recess, and Eddie could see Pat's bread truck parked in front of the small grocery store across from the tenement.

Later that morning, inside the bakery, Pat was marking up the order sheet for the next day's delivery. He glanced out the store window just in time to see two men in business suits entering Eddie's tenement foyer. Pat started to leave the shop. "Hey, Pat," Mrs. Antonelli, the woman behind the counter said. "Where you going? I haven't even paid you."

"I'll be right back," Pat said. "There's something I've got to take care of."

Mrs. Antonelli shook her head in dismay and spoke into the abandoned shop. "They get crazier every day around here."

Pat jumped in his truck, drove up the street to the coffee shop, and double-parked. He ran into the shop and spotted Tony behind the counter.

"Did Eddie leave?" Pat asked.

"Yeah, he left about ten minutes ago. He and Mario."

"Did he say where he was going?" Pat glanced around.

"No, why? What's up?" Tony said.

"Oh, nothin' much." A frown clouded his face. "I just need to see him."

Pat jumped back in his truck and headed down the street looking for Eddie and Mario. He stopped at the next corner where a bunch of guys were gathered.

Pat leaned out the window of the truck. "Anybody seen Eddie?"

"Yeah," one of them replied, "we just saw him and Mario." Another guy added, "I think they were on their way to The Club."

"Great. Thanks," Pat said and accelerated off to The Club. He double-parked and ran up to the metal door and rang the bell. The panel slid open.

"Hey, Buddy, is Eddie in there?" Pat questioned.

Buddy opened the door slightly. "Yeah, come on in, Pat."

"No, I'm in a hurry. I'll wait out here," Pat said, leaning in the doorway. "Could you tell Eddie I want to see him...It's kinda important."

"Sure," Buddy answered, quietly shutting the door, clicking the lock into place.

Pat paced up and down. Finally the door flew open and Eddie stepped out with a worried look.

"What's up Pat?"

"You're not in any jam, are you?" Pat asked.

"No, not that I know of, why?" Eddie said blinking in the daylight.

"Are you telling me straight?" Pat asked.

"Hey Pat...what are you driving at? I'm not in any trouble. What's the problem?"

"I just saw two detective-looking types go into your building. You sure you're not in a jam?" Pat asked again.

Eddie hesitated and tried to remember anything recent enough.

"No, I'm telling you, I haven't done anything," Eddie insisted. "Are you sure they went in my building?"

"I'm sure," Pat responded, chewing his lip.

"Give me a ride home, will you?" Eddie asked. "I'll tell Mario and be right back."

Eddie disappeared for a few seconds and then came out and bounded into the delivery truck. Pat drove quickly to the tenement.

"You want me to come in with you, or wait?" Pat asked, looking up at the front doors to the tenement. "I didn't like the looks of them. Cops or something. You know what I mean?"

"I know what you mean," Eddie replied, scanning the street for an unmarked police car. "But don't worry about it."

"I'll be at the store across the street if you need me," Pat said.

Eddie entered the tenement cautiously. Nunzio was playing at the bottom of the stairway in the foyer.

"Hey, Nunzio, did you see two men in suits come in here?"

"Yeah, I saw one go into Mr. Lazzaro's apartment," Nunzio pointed upward. "The other one came back down and went out...."

Eddie hurried up the stairs and knocked on Mr. Lazzaro's door.

"Eddie, come in, come in. What? No work today?" Mr. Lazzaro greeted him and led him into the parlor. "Look who came for a visit this morning!"

It was Joe Angelino. Eddie wondered, *Why didn't Pat recognize Joe as one of the suspicious characters?* Maybe it was his fancy suit. Joe was dressed in his best pinstriped suit and stood up to shake hands with Eddie. Eddie hesitated.

"Oh come on, you two," Mr. Lazzaro said. "I've been refereeing your fights since you played stick ball on the street out front. Shake... come on, Eddie."

Eddie shook his hand and stared into Joe's steady gaze.

"Now, sit down, you two," Mr. Lazzaro ordered. "We were just talking about the City's 'agenda,' as Angel puts it."

"Now, Mr. Lazzaro," Angel reprimanded. "It should be all our agenda. This business of redevelopment has been negotiated for years. Since Eddie and I were in eighth grade at least."

"Actually, I've been hearing this idea since before that," Mr. Lazzaro said. "You see, after I first came to America, the Yankees and Irish were always complaining about the Italian slums. Can you imagine the nerve of the Irish, after all they went through? Ha!"

"It's just part of the assimilation process. I studied this at Harvard," Angel said. "I even wrote some parts of the study that went into the final federal grant request."

"That's just great, Angel," Eddie said. "You betray your people for a stupid shot at a job from Harvard."

"Hey, this finally has nothing to do with Harvard," Angel countered.

"Gimme a break! You know everybody with clout has a finger in this," Eddie said.

Angel hesitated and looked at Mr. Lazzaro, who said nothing but waited.

"Look, this isn't getting us anywhere," Angel said. "The fact is, the West End is going through a major change, a complete transformation. Traumatic as that is, in the long run it will be a healthier, cleaner community."

"Bull!" Eddie grumbled.

"Now, Eddie, hear Angel out. He's made a special trip here. I'm honored he took the time to show respect."

"Okay, okay, so let's hear the bad news and get it over with so we can put you out of business," Eddie said.

Angel took a deep breath and sighed. "Okay, before you came I was trying to explain to Mr. Lazzaro that the property in this area has been taken over by the City under eminent domain...and I was explaining what that is. But I don't think I'm getting this across too well."

"No, you're doing fine," Mr. Lazzaro clarified. "I just don't want to sell my building, that's all."

"That's simple enough," Eddie said. "He doesn't want to sell it."

"But didn't all of you receive letters from the Boston Redevelopment Authority stating their policies?"

"Yes, we did," Eddie said. "So what? You think we kiss every bureaucrat's behind just because we get a letter on official stationery?"

"Look," Angel said, getting a little flushed. "I came here to talk with Mr. Lazzaro...not you. I'll deal with you separately."

"Yeah," Eddie said. "I bet you will. I can't wait for that meeting."

"Now, let's cut this out, boys," Mr. Lazzaro said. "Say what you have to say, Angel."

"Quite simply," Angel said, sitting forward, opening a copy of the letter to Mr. Lazzaro. "The City will be purchasing your building under eminent domain. And, given the condition and age of the building, the purchase price will probably run about ten percent of the building's original cost."

"Jesus," Eddie half stood up, and leaned forward slapping the letter in Angel's hand. "It's worth a lot more than that to Mr. Lazzaro and the rest of us."

"I don't think you understand. This is not negotiable, really. This building has been effectively purchased under the law of eminent domain."

Mr. Lazzaro sat back and rolled his eyes to the ceiling.

Eddie was nearly shouting. "I think it's you who doesn't understand. Mr. Lazzaro has worked most of his life to own this building. He's the legal owner. He treats his tenants like family, always has...or have you forgotten? He has always kept the rents low...why do you think he's still hustling fish down on the pier? For God's sake, Angel!"

"Hey, enough Eddie," Mr. Lazzaro said. He reddened and sat forward. "Quiet now for a minute."

"I think the City is making a fair price offer for these tenements," Angel insisted.

Mr. Lazzaro raised his hand for silence. "Now, Angel, you know me. I will think about these things you have said."

Angel sat quietly looking at Mr. Lazzaro.

"I want to tell you that we haven't decided how to react to this news," Mr. Lazzaro said. "It's coming so suddenly...but don't think we won't have a plan of our own. I appreciate your position. I know you're doing what you think is best. But it's not what I want. I've lived here for too many years and I, and a lot of others, don't want to start all over. Ca-peesh?"

Angel folded the letter and put it inside his coat pocket. He stood up with Mr. Lazzaro and shook his hand.

"Another day, then," Angel said to him. "I'm sorry this seems so hard. It doesn't have to be. Another day I'll share with you our plans for elderly residents. We offer alternative housing transition planning, and..."

"I think you've made your point, Angel," Eddie said. "Why don't you get the heck out of here!"

Mr. Lazzaro tugged at Eddie's arm and shook his head in disapproval. He then guided Angel to the door. Eddie stepped out into the hallway with Angel while he said goodbye to Mr. Lazzaro.

After the door closed, Angel started to turn away, but Eddie grabbed him and whirled him around.

"How can you put a price tag on an old man's property, his home, my home?" Eddie demanded to know. "What kind of man have you become? You come to this man's home and you offer him close to nothing for this building. You have the balls to tell him the City has bought his home... and mine, and everyone else' in the West End. You can't take our homes. This is the United States of America. This is our home!" Eddie yelled a few inches from Angel's unmoved face. "Mr. Lazzaro worked his whole life for this...this is his retirement income. Just who do you think you are?"

Angel assumed an authoritative tone. "Hey, I don't have to take this abuse. I'm here on official City business. The deal is this, Eddie. You, Mr. Lazzaro, and everyone else in this building will have to pay rent to the City until it's time to move out prior to demolition. If you don't pay the rent, you'll face eviction. It's that simple."

Eddie grabbed Angel by his jacket and shoved him to the top step.

"Hey! Just a minute!" Angel shouted.

Doors below opened and heads popped out. Anna appeared behind Eddie.

"Take your hands off me, Eddie!" Angel said.

"You got a lot of nerve, Angel. I oughta throw your butt down the stairs. You and the other City crooks better keep your distance. Don't come back here again. The next time I won't be so nice."

"You're really scaring me," Angel said and laughed as Eddie released him. Knowing Anna was watching, Eddie straightened Angel's coat and tie.

"Take care, Angel," Eddie whispered close to his ear and then gave him a gentle push toward the stairs.

"Eddie!" Anna shouted from behind him. "What's going on? What's all the yelling about?"

"Joe the Death Angel Angelino, our big college grad, is here trying to cheat Mr. Lazzaro out of his building!" Eddie shouted down the stairs. Other residents booed as Angel descended the stairs quickly.

"Where is Mr. Lazzaro?" Anna inquired. She was almost in tears, and Catharine on her hip, wide-eyed and upset by all the noise, began to cry.

"He's in his apartment," Eddie replied.

Anna went across the hall and knocked on Mr. Lazzaro's door. He let them in and slowly eased down in his rocker and sighed. Anna knelt on the floor in front of him.

"Well, this is a gray day, isn't it?" Mr. Lazzaro commented. "I wonder if they can really take the building away so fast?"

"Oh, I don't think so," Anna said.

"Of course not," Eddie agreed.

Mr. Lazzaro took Catharine from Anna. "I'm glad my wife didn't live to see this mess," Mr. Lazzaro said. "Eddie, take it easy with Angel. Don't be so hot headed. There are better ways, believe me. In a few days, we'll map out our own strategy...okay?"

After a short visit with Mr. Lazzaro, Eddie and Anna returned to their apartment. Anna put Catharine in her high chair and started feeding her a jar of baby food. Eddie saw Anna was crying softly.

"You got fired, didn't you?" she asked.

Eddie sat down across from her. "Yeah...laid off. Fired. Whatever. I didn't want to worry you, especially with all the other stuff. Mario and I were out looking for work when this business with Angel came up...Jesus!"

"So many bad things are happening all at once. What will we do now?" Anna asked.

"Look, don't worry. I'll find something," Eddie replied. He went around the table and hugged her.

"Eddie, I think we should seriously consider moving...if my parents move to Medford or wherever. My father could help us get started again."

"Look, Anna, I know this is upsetting," Eddie said. "But let me be clear. We're not moving. We won't have to. I guarantee that. There are things we can do."

"But they just might take our home. Then what?" Anna asked.

Eddie squatted down by her chair and held her hand.

"Look, I promise you...PROMISE, okay? This is a lot of bull. I've lived here all my life. This is my home. And what about all these old people? These people came from Italy. They got off the boat and they came right here, a couple of blocks from the boat. Like Mr. Lazzaro, Aunt Lucy, Luigi. So did the Irish. And did they get their neighborhoods torn down? No! They're still here in the city. And the Italians will be no different."

Eddie stood up and paced the kitchen like a caged lion.

"It really fries me that you're having doubts, that you want to give up so easily." He stood facing her, a sudden rush of anger getting a strong hold of him.

"Eddie, calm down," Anna said.

"No, no, wait a minute, Anna, we shouldn't even be having this conversation. I'm really disappointed. You should know how I feel about living here."

"Well, I grew up in the West End too," she pointed out.

"Yeah, well you didn't grow up in one building with the same people. You moved around, here and there. Your Dad was all over the place."

"Don't start with my father," Anna warned. "Or we talk about your Dad and all his trouble."

"I'm not starting anything." Eddie pulled back some hard things he wanted to say. "But get this straight. We're not leaving here. And no letter or Joe Angelino or Mayor Cowley can make that happen if we fight it. You want to stay in this family, you gotta be a fighter, not a victim. You fight, you don't run!"

"Well maybe I like being a victim. Maybe I'm tired of the West End," Anna exclaimed.

Eddie stood staring at her in total dismay. "I can't believe we're having this conversation!" he shouted. Catharine began to squall. Anna jumped up.

"Screw this!" Eddie shouted. "I'm going to The Club to look for work. I don't need this!"

"Oh, a great place to look for work. Julia and her gang!" Anna said. "Why not the unemployment office?"

Eddie came up to her and she drew back as he pulled out a roll of money from his pocket.

"You worried about money? Don't! My friends here in the West End look out for each other. So here," he said. "Here's some money to keep you from crying." He threw a hundred dollar bill on the table. Anna's eyes widened in shock.

Eddie jabbed his finger at her, "I really don't need this." Then he grabbed his jacket and stormed out of the apartment, slamming the door, and pounding down the stairway. Anna broke into tears and hugged and rocked Catharine.

"Well, maybe we don't need this either," she said, kissing the baby on the forehead.

8

THE BOSS

Eddie spent the afternoon at The Club playing cards and drinking beers with Mario and the regular crowd. By dinnertime, he was feeling a little tipsy, so he ordered a cold cut sandwich. He kept playing and losing at poker until almost nine. Mario had already left and returned after running several errands for The Club.

"Wow, you're still here," he said to Eddie. "What's with you? You have a fight with Anna?"

Eddie tried to focus his eyes on his cards and glanced over at Mario with a blank, poker face. "Leave Anna out of this," he said, his tongue feeling slow.

"Ahhh..." Mario said. "I see...something, but not a fight."

Eddie mumbled. "What we need is work. W-O-R-K...You got me?"

"Oh boy, don't tell me you want to answer ads in *The Globe*?"

Several of the guys chuckled.

"No, not that," Eddie said. "Maybe another something for Buddy. Go talk to him."

Mario perked up. "Wow, I can't believe my ears. Just the other day..."

"Never mind the other day. Tonight..." Eddie said, sitting up straight and playing a card, "tonight is different."

"Hey, you're the boss. I'll talk to him," Mario said. "But first let's have some coffee. Joe, a couple of black coffees over here!"

Eddie finished his hand and sipped the steaming hot coffee cautiously. Mario drank his coffee quickly and disappeared into the office area. He returned a little later.

"So?" Eddie prompted.

"So, settle up here and we take a ride," Mario winked.

"Hey, I'm in no shape for something tonight," Eddie said, getting up slowly, shaking his hands all around. He was down to less than two hundred bucks now.

"Don't worry," Mario whispered and took Eddie by the arm. "We're just going to have a little meeting."

"Where?"

"Never you mind. It's a little surprise," Mario said. "It's gonna be like old home week."

Eddie squinted at Mario suspiciously. They took a car parked next to The Club that everyone used for errands around town. Mario drove a couple of blocks and pulled over in front of a set of West End three-deckers.

"What are we stopping for?" Eddie asked, looking out at the deserted sidewalk.

"You're getting out here. I got my orders from the boss's boss," Mario said seriously. "Number twelve, second floor. You're expected. I gotta run and get a guy at the airport. Be back by midnight. You'll probably walk home before that, so, I'll see you tomorrow. Then we can talk about the deal."

"Goddammit," Eddie said. "I don't like this!"

"Hey," Mario replied with a laugh. "Would I drop you off here if I didn't have a pleasant surprise for you...huh?" Mario gave him a gentle push. "Now get out and get up to number twelve second floor."

Eddie shook his head. What was he doing? As soon as he'd asked for this line of work, strange things started happening. He trusted Mario, but what the...? He crawled from the car and leaned in the window.

"Okay, man, but I hope you're not wasting my time."

"Get going, will ya...Jesus, what a suspicious character you are," Mario said. Then as he pulled away, he yelled, "Be good!"

Eddie went in the ground floor of the apartments and tried unsuccessfully to read the name inked on a torn card in the mailbox numbered twelve. Giving up, he climbed the stairs, straightened his jacket and shirt, and ran his fingers through his hair as he stood before the door. Then he knocked and waited. He had the distinct feeling he was being watched, but there was no peephole in the door. Suddenly, he could hear music playing in the distance, the shuffling of footsteps, and the door being unchained in several places.

The door finally squeaked open and there was Julia Tocci, the daughter of Carlos Tocci, the boss of all the rackets in the inner city.

"So Eddie Sveglio! Aren't you a sight for sore eyes!" Julia said, waving him in. "I didn't know if you'd make it. Buddy said you were having a pretty good time at The Club."

Julia, slim and curvaceous as always, was dressed in tight black pants, silver slippers and a bright red blouse with a ruffled front. Her jet black hair was done up in a pony tail and frosted, her makeup liberally applied to her olive-toned skin. She followed him down the dark hallway into an ultra-modern living room of chrome and glass, with peacock feathers in crystal decanters and prints of abstract reds and yellows on the wall.

"Sit down," she said, indicating a large leather sofa. A white Persian cat stood up, stretched, and jumped to the thick blue carpet. "You like cats, don't you? I remember you liked my other cats when I lived at home. This one's Liz, named after Liz Taylor. She's one of my favorite actresses. Look, you want anything before we get started?"

"Where are the others?" Eddie asked.

"What others? I'm the others," she laughed. "You don't know? Who do you think handles the West End? A girl's gotta have something to do."

"You mean your Dad gave you The Club to run? Buddy--"

"Buddy smuddy! You've really been out of touch." Julia laughed and sat down next to him on the sofa. "I guess marriage does things to you, huh?"

Eddie looked at Julia and frowned. They had dated in high school and for a brief time there had been an intense love affair after they graduated. But Julia had her agenda—her father, and Eddie had his—his mother. And his mother wanted nothing to do with Julia Tocci. He could hear her now, fuming in the kitchen, ranting against his affair with her. "That Julia Tocci is a spoiled rich girl. There's only one man in her life— her father. She'll drop you like a hat, anytime. I'm tellin' you, Eddie...you listenin' to me?" Remembering, Eddie couldn't restrain a smile.

"So what's so funny?" Julia questioned. "Anna tell you not to talk to me?"

"Leave Anna out of this."

"I swear, I thought she was gonna be a nun," Julia said. "Surprised me she ever knew what to do. What an innocent lamb... you know what I mean?"

Eddie folded his hands and waited. Julia fell silent.

"Are you finished?" Eddie said. "It's over between us, okay. I'm married. I got a daughter to think about."

"So I heard," Julia sighed. "I'll have to stop by and give her a little gift."

"That's okay," Eddie said. "Let's get down to business."

"Hey, whatever you want," Julia said. She pulled out a cigarette from a Chinese lacquered box on the glass coffee table and offered Eddie one.

"No thanks."

"Oh, I forgot. You've given up all your bad vices."

Eddie sighed and leaned back in the folds of the sofa and waited. Julia lit her cigarette and blew a jet of smoke in the air.

"Okay, so down to business," she said. "So, you want some light work with your buddy Mario—Pretty Boy. Everybody's glad you'll be out there with Mario. Mario's a nice guy and all that, but you know, he misses a few notes here and there."

"What do you mean?" Eddie asked.

"Nothing really. You know, he goofs around, he's not as serious as you."

"Pretty Boy can handle the heavy stuff too."

"Good. I like to think of him having a partner, level headed," Julia said. "Somebody to help handle the money. Sometimes the payroll...jeez, it gets a little careless down at The Club. Buddy's no Price Waterhouse either, you know. Don't get me wrong, though. Buddy's got our full endorsement, don't underestimate that."

"I never had any doubts," Eddie said.

"Now, occasionally, you know, there're these pickups and errands that need doing," Julia explained while tapping her cigarette. "Sometimes little things, sometimes, well, big things. And the pay runs commensurate with the trouble. There's a thing coming up, a pretty big thing. We're always glad nobody gets hurt. We don't want anyone to get hurt, of course."

"Of course," Eddie said.

Julia edged a little closer and her knee pushed against his leg. Eddie gave her a direct, questioning look.

"So," Julia whispered, drawing closer. "I have to talk low in case there are any little ears. I mean, you never know these days."

"Uh huh," said Eddie, playing along.

"Thing is we'd like to help you out from time to time," she said in a soft voice. "I mean you're a family man now. You got to think of three instead of one or even two. Who knows, maybe more eventually, right? But people are wondering about your commitment. You know, how far are you willing to go? All the way? Or just enough to be a gofer?"

"For now, I want to stick with the errands," Eddie said. "The partner stuff with Mario will be just fine."

"I see."

"Just a little extra money to hold me until I find a better job," Eddie made clear.

"Or a job at all, huh?" Julia said. "I heard about the 'factory layoff', I think Mario called it."

"Well, don't you know everything," Eddie replied, feeling his face become warm with embarrassment.

"Sweetie, you don't have any idea," Julia patted him on the arm.

"So do you have anything or is this just smoke and mirrors?" Eddie smiled.

"Oh, wise guy still," Julia laughed. "Well, okay, how about this?" She leaned across him and kissed him on the lips with an open mouth. He started to resist, but let go, and she almost crawled on top of him. "Oh, Eddie, I've missed this so much," she said, tightening her arm around his neck. He finally twisted free.

"Had enough, Julia," he shook his head. "You're just jerking me around, right?"

"No, Eddie, no."

Eddie sat forward. "Listen, it's over between us. It was great way back when, but things have changed. I'm married now. I've got others to think of. Anyway, I heard you were serious with Johnny Scuro."

"That doesn't change your heart, Eddie. Johnny...he's nice, you know, for an escort, but he's playing gofer for Nero. I think he wants to be governor or something, for God's sake."

"So Johnny won't be your gofer. You'll find someone else, huh? Give me a break. You haven't been interested in me since we broke up. You've been dating half the gang working for your father."

"Oh really?" Julia wondered, almost joyously. "So you do keep tabs on me?"

"Hell no," Eddie said. "Just get real. I need a freakin' part time job. Nothing heavy-duty, okay? I'm not lookin' to retire just yet."

"You could've gone a long way with my father," Julia reminded him.

Eddie looked at her straight on. "Yeah, sure, I could be dead, too."

"Oh, don't be so dramatic!" Julia retorted. "You watch too many stupid movies."

Eddie shook his head. "Look, this is like an old record I hear playing, you and me fighting again. Forget it. Let's just be friends. That's best for us, okay?" He got up from the sofa and started for the door. Julia ran around him and put her arms around his waist.

"Eddie," she whispered. "Eddie, I need your help. There are things you could do for me, for my father. Important things. Worth a lot of money. You understand?"

Eddie pried her arms away.

"Julia, I came for a business meeting...what is this?"

"Okay, Eddie. Okay. Here, here's an advance." She stuffed money in his jacket pocket. "There's five hundred more. Five hundred for a job with Mario. This week. He'll get the word. Are you happy now?" Julia asked. "You wanna be small time, that's your business."

"I don't want to make a living being a wise guy," Eddie said, gripping her by the shoulders. "You gotta understand that. You tell your father as well. A few errands and then I'm legit again."

Julia laughed. "Wow, I guess you never loved me a bit, did you? It was always pretend. See what you can get off Julia?"

"You know that's not true," Eddie said quietly. "We were in high school. It's different now. I've gotta think about my future and family responsibilities."

"Sure, sure, Eddie," Julia half agreed and shook her head matter-of-factly. "Go on. Hurry home. Give my love to Anna and the baby."

"Hey, Julia, ease up, why don't you?" Eddie said giving her a quick kiss on the cheek. "We're all facing bigger problems now."

"Maybe you Eddie. Me, well, I'm your age too and you see what I've got—." Julia waved at her apartment. "Nobody here."

"Come on, Julia, you're feeling sorry for yourself," Eddie said. "You know you got guys chasing you. I hear the talk."

"Yeah, chasing me, for what?" Julia pointed out. "My money? Or...you know."

Eddie frowned. "Listen, unless we get busy, we may all lose the West End. What's your father saying about that?"

"I don't want to talk about Boston politics," Julia said. "Don't you want to stay for a while?" She moved next to him and wrapped her arm around his waist.

Eddie was shocked. He wanted her again. He wanted to grab Julia and pull her down on the carpet and make love to her again, like the time on the rooftop, but he drew himself back and took a breath.

Julia smiled. "Ahhh, I thought the old Eddie was still around here somewhere."

"Hey, you're still a beautiful woman. You're still Julia Tocci. But I gotta go," Eddie insisted. "I'm just not available anymore. I'll be back in touch after Mario and I do this errand for you."

"Okay, old man," she quipped back, smiling triumphantly. "But don't try to reach me. I'll be in touch through Buddy at The Club. You'll hear from me first, sweetie." She leaned forward, gave him another brief kiss on the lips and, opening the door, she pushed him out playfully.

"Later, lover boy," she said.

"Unbelievable," Eddie groaned as he made his way down the stairs, wiping off the lipstick from his cheek and lips.

He walked around the streets for half an hour, clearing his head, then he went home, showered, and climbed into bed next to Anna.

Eddie checked his watch. It was close to 4 AM. He took a deep breath and exhaled a long plume of white mist. He stretched and cracked his twenty-three year old back, limbering up. On the narrow West End Street and over the tenement rooftops, the early morning fog obscured the skyline of downtown Boston. For a moment, he almost lost a sense of where he was. Then he shook himself.

He spotted the van cruising slowly up the narrow street toward him. He was fairly sure it was Mario, Mr. Pretty Boy, of the movie ambitions. "Star quality," Mario once said. "I'm looking for star quality." He'd see stars if he didn't stick to business.

Mario had said it would be a borrowed van, one with plates that could be lost. As it drew closer, he could see the dented front and the paint scraped from the side. What a piece of junk.

The van slowed down and pulled to the curb in front of the three-decker tenement steps. Eddie dug his hands into his workout jacket and stepped forward. The fogged window rolled down slightly and a middle finger entered the blank space.

"Hey, you sleepy *sonofa*!" a familiar voice said. "Nice way to take a day off from work. Are you nuts or what?"

The window came the rest of the way down revealing Mario's broad smile. "Get in."

Eddie jogged around the van and climbed in.

"Hate to roust you outta bed with the old lady," Mario said, lurching forward into first gear. "Course I'll be glad to take your place."

"You jerk," Eddie laughed. "Where'd you get this piece of crap? More of Buddy's chop shop specials?"

"Who cares? A quickie like this and you and me split a grand. Must be something smokin' hot coming off that boat. Here, I brought you a coffee."

They drove out of the West End's narrow winding streets and lurched down the artery toward downtown. A newspaper truck passed them, then a cop car.

"Be cool, be cool." Mario began whistling.

"Hey Einstein, it's on the way back you don't want to be stopped. You get stopped now, we're just running an errand for Buddy. It's his problem the plates don't check out."

"Ooooh, uptight as usual," Mario said. "Married life must be gettin' to you."

"I'm not tired of married life," Eddie said bluntly, "I'm tired of playing two-bit gofer for extra dough. There's a better way, gotta be."

"Oooh," Mario said, "me the still single dude, having a ball. And you, an old worried man."

"Just wait, pal, just wait. You'll see."

Mario laughed. "You won't catch me taking the big leap. Not unless I gotta. Oh, I'm sorry, Eddie. Me and my big mouth. Jesus!"

Eddie blew his breath over the coffee and looked out at the city looming through the fog.

"Forget it, man. Anna was already planning the wedding when she got pregnant with Catharine. The important thing is you love the person," Eddie pointed out.

"Yeah, I haven't gotten lucky in that department yet."

"So what's the plan?" Eddie asked. "They just give us this stuff, right? We drive off, quick and dirty?"

"Well, close, I think," Mario said, sounding a little confused. "Buddy gave me a password. Said the guy's expecting the two goons from the McGrath gang to do the pickup. We're just arriving a little ahead of them. Apparently the old man McGrath is down on his luck and holding out. So you know how it is."

Eddie shook his head. "I see, a little garnishee through trade in kind. Don't pay up and sharks gobble your assets."

"Yeah, that's about it," Mario acknowledged.

"So we're the little sharks. Better hope this deal's timed right."

"Buddy said it's a cinch," said Mario. "We'll be here at least an hour before the McGraths. Hey, I'm not worried. I'm just the dumb driver." Mario laughed and poked Eddie in the shoulder. "You're the hero, remember?"

"Thanks a lot, as usual..."

Mario turned down a narrow street and bumped along a wharf toward a warehouse.

"It's Number 170, Gate B. Where the heck is it?" Mario groaned and lurched forward creeping through the heavy fog. "I can't see a thing!"

"Don't panic," Eddie said as he wiped the windshield with a rag. "Try down there, around the corner. Slower."

The van eased down the docks. Mario turned the van and the headlights swept across the rusted warehouse loading doors.

"There it is," Eddie said. "Pull up and back up to the main door, just like we're all business."

Mario's hands were shaking slightly. He shifted into neutral and revved up the engine. "Gee, try reverse for a change," Mario suggested. He laughed nervously and slapped his forehead. The old van chugged back toward the loading door.

"Okay, what now?" Eddie asked.

"You go up to the office door and the clerk will be waiting. Just whisper the password and that's it."

"No paperwork? No nothin'?" Eddie asked in disbelief.

"Yeah, just the password, that's it. Simple as pie."

"Right. So?" Eddie questioned.

"So what?" Mario said.

"So what's the password?"

Mario looked at Eddie for a second with a blank look on his face.

"Oh no, Mary protect us." Eddie groaned. "You forgot!"

"Something, some city over in— No, just pulling your leg, got it written right here on my wrist. Just in case I forgot." Mario pulled up his sleeve and held his wrist under the lights from the dashboard. Printed in blue ballpoint ink was the word "DUBLIN."

"DUBLIN!" Eddie laughed. "Should have known. So brother McGrath, let's get the merchandise. Leave the engine running."

They went up to the metal side door and Eddie gave it a rap and waited. Mario shook himself from the chill. The fog was thick and there was no sign of the morning light. Eddie gave the door another, louder knock.

"Where's the guy?" Mario asked.

"Shh, remember, we're early," Eddie whispered.

There was a sound from the other side, like metal being dragged against concrete. A deep guttural voice came through the door's frame.

"Who's there?"

"McGrath," Eddie answered. "Let's get movin'..."

"You're early."

"Open the door or you'll have to answer to my boss, jerk," Eddie shouted.

There was a pause. "What's the password?" the voice came again.

"Dublin," Eddie replied.

There was another longer pause. "That ain't the dumb password. Who are you guys?"

Eddie looked at Mario, whose eyes were rolling.

"Hell," Mario said. "Buddy can't remember squat!"

Eddie shook his head in frustration.

"We better get outta here," Mario said. "Man, I'm sorry. What a big mess."

"I need the money and I ain't leavin' without the stuff," Eddie told Mario. "We're here and we're gonna get the job done."

"How?"

"Hey!" Eddie shouted at the doorkeeper. "Open this stupid door. Dublin, mumblin'...somebody messed up. Not us. You don't open up, we come in, and it won't be pretty. The Boss doesn't like to wait."

There was silence.

"I think I better make a call," the voice said again.

"You pick up that phone and we're comin' in after you. Don't mess with us. Open the door, NOW!"

Eddie backed up and kicked the steel door with full force.

"Get the gun outta the truck. I'm tired of this creep!"

Mario opened the rear door of the van and shut it for effect. After a brief pause, the door locks sounded slowly. The door eased open. The man was huge. He took one look and his face lit up with surprise.

"Hey, who are you guys?"

Eddie with a swift, clean move grabbed the longshoreman by the collar and threw him out the door to the pavement. Eddie then pinned him down.

"Don't ever give us trouble again," Eddie said, pulling the cursing guy's arm behind him.

"You're not the McGrath guys! Who are you?"

"Get up," Eddie demanded, pulling him to his feet. "Check inside," he motioned to Mario.

Mario scrambled in the door and found the switch to open the loading bay. It ground slowly upward.

"It's piled right here by the door," said Mario. "I can get it, I think."

Mario groaned and shoved the box toward the van.

"I think I'll need some help getting this in. It's a heavy mother."

"You guys are dead, you know that," the longshoreman said.

"'Scuse me," Eddie said to Mario. "I better talk to our friend here."

Mario watched as Eddie walked the heavyset man over to the wharf's edge. Eddie held the man's arm behind his back and appeared to whisper to him. Mario strained to hear.

"Screw you!" the guy shouted suddenly.

"Your choice, pal," Eddie said.

The man moaned, took a step, and jumped into the harbor water. There was a splash and Eddie trotted back to the van. They quickly loaded the box, jumped in the van, and started off.

"What did you say to him?" Mario asked. He laughed as they slipped up the street to the boulevard, heading back to the West End.

"Oh, I said we'd have to break his legs or he could take a swim," Eddie said. "I gave him a choice. Don't worry, he could dog paddle and there was a ladder within twenty feet. Keep movin'."

Eddie fingered the two medals hanging on the chain around his neck.

"Jesus," Mario whistled and laughed. "It's just like people say."

"What do you mean?"

"You're a chip off the old block. Your dad, I mean. He had a rep like this—one tough, street-smart dude."

"Yeah, well, my old man never had to raise a family either."

"Whaddaya mean?"

"He died in the war at Normandy. I was four, can't really remember him. I only know about him through what the old timers tell me.

"I never knew that," Mario admitted.

Eddie touched the medals around his neck.

"That's his bronze star you're wearing," Mario said. "I forgot about all that And the other one?"

"Oh, that's my First Communion medal, Saint Joseph. Mr. Lazzaro gave it to me."

Mario sighed and laughed. "You're out there...wow!"

"You're not so bad yourself." Eddie laughed and shoved Mario gently. "Next time get the open sesame right."

"Hey, I swear...," Mario said, holding his hands up in protest.

"Never mind, we'll take it up with Buddy and the gang. Drop me off at Gino's. I'll meet you at The Club later and settle up."

9

COLUMBUS DAY

Columbus Day was a beautiful, clear day, unseasonably warm for October. A gentle wind swept off the harbor. The traditional West End festival at the Holy Name Parish Church was normally held indoors, but with the nice weather this year, the guests would be able to enjoy the church supper outside in the courtyard. By late afternoon, swarms of residents of all ages were enjoying the festivities.

Children were running around playing tag, while on a small stage the Roma Band played Italian marches. Heaps of food, wine, and sodas weighed down the rows of long tables covered in bright checkered tablecloths. American and Italian flags flapped in the breezes that swayed the shade trees. Behind them in the distance hovered the tall buildings of the financial district in downtown Boston.

Eddie, Anna, Catharine, and the other tenement dwellers sat together at the same table. They ate, laughed, and joked. Everyone was in a festive mood except for Mr. Lazzaro. He seemed slightly withdrawn.

Anna's father, Casimo, poured out another glass of wine for Mr. Lazzaro.

"What a turn out! There are so many people; just like old times, huh, Mr. Lazzaro?"

"Yes, just like old times," Mr. Lazzaro nodded without smiling.

"Everyone seems so friendly. It makes me feel good," Anna said.

Mr. Lazzaro's old chum Luigi swayed over to the table. He had arrived in Boston from Italy the same year as Mr. Lazzaro. Tonight he was enjoying his wine.

"*Ciao*, Joseph," he shouted above the band music to Mr. Lazzaro. "*Ciao*, Eddie, Anna."

They all raised their glasses in greeting.

"Look at all these people!" Luigi said with a flourish of his arm. He leaned over to Mr. Lazzaro and whispered, "My old friend, did you perhaps bring your wine?"

Mr. Lazzaro smiled and reached under the table. He brought out a gallon jug of his red wine.

"Oh, that's great. A little later, we'll have a game of bocce and some more of this wonderful creation," Luigi said.

Mr. Lazzaro hesitated after pouring and capped the wine bottle.

"Sure, why don't you, Mr. Lazzaro?" Eddie asked.

"*Sí, sí*," Mr. Lazzaro said, patting his old friend on the arm.

"I'll see you later," Luigi said. "It's my turn cooking sausages."

"Hey, they're starting the feast," Eddie announced. "Let's go. Let's go, everybody."

They all got up from the table and congregated where the food was being served. They filed through the line, piling their plates with food in rhythm with the lively Italian march. As they passed Luigi, he served out the steaming sausages, onions and peppers, singing along.

As the daylight faded, the colored lights came on across the courtyard, illuminating the area with a soft light. Eddie spotted a long black hearse parked in front of the courtyard. Emerging from its depths was State Representative Antonio Nero, rotund and resplendent in his decorous black suit. He also doubled as the local funeral director. He walked through the crowd, shaking hands and shouting hellos. Following in his wake was his smiling wife, his family, and his associates.

Mario appeared at the table and slipped into a spot near Mr. Lazzaro. Anna poured him some wine.

"Well, here comes the grave digger, old Nero," Mario said. "Wonder what he's looking for, customers or votes? Jeez, his re-election is over a year away."

"Never hurts to mingle with the people," Anna said.

Nero passed near their table and waved. As he paused with a group of voters, Johnny Scuro, his top associate, whispered in his ear and Nero turned slightly. Looking at Eddie, he smiled knowingly and nodded. Eddie nodded in return. Then Nero made his way to the bandstand where they were setting up a lectern for him.

Johnny signaled for the band to stop playing.

"Boy, that Johnny," Mario said. "He's got himself one helluva job."

"And, I hear, quite a few girlfriends," Casimo remarked.

Anna looked at her sisters and mother and smiled. "Oh, Dad," she said, "now you're keeping up with the dating game in the neighborhood."

"Nah," Casimo responded, sighing. "You women calm down. You know how the women are always chasing us good-looking guys, right Eddie?" Casimo turned to look at Eddie.

"You bet," Eddie agreed. He glanced at Anna who was not smiling.

"Well, I hear he's going around with Julia Tocci," Anna said flatly.

"Whoa!" Mario said. "Anna, you must have the second sight. Speak of the devil Look who's over there with him by the bandstand."

Mario looked at Eddie and shrugged.

Julia was, in fact, hanging on Johnny's arm. Johnny gave her a kiss and went up on the bandstand.

"Good evening, I hope you're enjoying yourself," Johnny said.

Cheers rang out.

"Our friend, Representative Nero, needs no introduction. He has come to talk to us tonight about an important matter which concerns us all. Let's give him our attention for a few minutes, then we'll get back to the music. Thank you."

The crowd applauded, but a few boos could be heard.

"It's great to see all my good friends here today," the smiling Nero said. "This is the best community in Boston. I'm proud to be a part of it. I want to talk to you tonight about a serious matter. I think you all know what I'm talking about."

Nero raised his fist in mock anger.

"It's about the BRA, the Boston Redevelopment Agency. It's about the Mayor. and...," he paused, pulling out a letter from his coat and shaking it over the lectern. "And it's about these letters!"

The crowd jeered.

"I'll show you what I'm going to do with mine," he shouted. He began to tear it into pieces that fluttered like confetti over the crowd in front of the bandstand. "We know who's behind all this. It's the Mayor and his syndicate!" Then Nero bent his arm at the elbow with force, a gesture for "up yours,"—the Italian salute. He was greeted with much applause and hooting from the crowd.

71

"So, you know what the Mayor can do? You know what we're going to do? Who says we can't fight City Hall? Don't be frightened by these letters and the newspaper stories. They're just more of the Mayor's dirty tricks."

The crowd booed again loudly at the mention of the Mayor. Nero nodded his head in agreement and waited for the noise to die down.

"Now we've started a committee to save the West End, and I've asked a very influential business leader to lead it. I'd like you to listen to Mr. Bill Warren who has an important announcement to make. I want all you women and children to participate in a march with Mr. Warren to the Mayor's office, two weeks from this coming Monday. Unfortunately, I won't be able to make it. I have another meeting to attend."

"Ohhhh..." the crowd groaned.

"But Mr. Warren will lead you on. Okay, my dear friends, thank you for your continued support. Now, let me introduce Mr. Bill Warren."

Mr. Bill Warren, looking very much the upper class Bostonian Brahmin that he was, approached the podium.

"Thank you, Representative Nero. You're probably wondering what a Mayflower descendent is doing up here trying to save the Italian West End. Well, in short, I think our ethnic communities are beautiful. I think the West End is beautiful!"

The crowd shouted in agreement.

"That's right, and frankly, there's simply no necessary logic that proves the West End, or any other ethnic community in this city needs to go. But we all know that. Now we have to take action. Like Nero said, two weeks from Monday morning the committee will be sponsoring a Mother's March on City Hall. We would like all you women and your children to gather in front of the State House about 10 AM. From there, we'll march to City Hall and present our grievance against the so-called redevelopment of the West End. If there's a good turnout, the media will give us good coverage and the Mayor will wake up and listen. We all know how Mayor Cowley loves those votes!"

There was laughter, and boos directed at the Mayor.

"So, mothers and children, let me see you there. Thank you for your attention and have a happy evening!"

The band broke out into a noisy version of *Cuore Abruzzese.*

At the tenement table, Angelo turned to his wife, Rosa, and Anna and said, "So, are you gonna march? What about you Anna?"

Anna looked at Eddie for approval, who nodded okay. "Yes, I am! I think it's a good idea."

"Baby carriage and all?" Mario asked.

"Maybe if we stick together we can change the Mayor's mind," Eddie said.

"Yeah, but what good will a bunch of women with carriages do, marching on City Hall?" Mario raised his brow.

"They'll know we're not going to make it easy for them," Eddie replied.

"I'm not convinced anything is going to happen. Hey, what time is it?" Mario asked.

"Almost nine," Angelo said looking at his wristwatch.

Mario stood up and emptied his wine glass.

"Gotta super date. She's supposed to meet me here for the fireworks. Better go look for her. Hey, look over there!" Mario said pointed at Mr. Lazzaro, Luigi, and the other older men playing bocce. "This whole scheme must be scaring old-timers like Mr. Lazzaro, eh?"

"I don't think it is. Don't underestimate Mr. Lazzaro. He's tougher than you will ever know," Eddie said.

"Yeah, guess you're right. Well, I'll be back after I gig and gag with my chick."

Mario winked at Anna, who rolled her eyes.

"See you later."

"Look at Mr. Lazzaro," Anna said. "Looks like he's having some fun now."

"Looks like he's forgotten his troubles," Eddie mentioned. "It just isn't fair. A guy like him works his whole life to own his home and then the City comes along and tells him they own it. Unbelievable, this eminent domain stuff."

"Underneath," Angelo said softly, "we're all upset."

Angelo's son Nunzio and another boy ran playfully around the table disrupting the adults' conversation.

"Nunzio, stop screaming and go play near the grass where there aren't so many people," Angelo shouted. He continued. "You know, it's a shame, this redevelopment thing. What in the world do they expect us to do? They send us an eviction notice and tell us to move out," Angelo said.

"Yeah, we've been here for twenty years. Anna was born here in the West End," Casimo reminded them.

73

"Hey," Eddie said, "let's take it one step at a time. We're not out in the street yet. Let's forget it for now. Anna, can you pour me some more of Mr. Lazzaro's wine? Thanks."

Eddie took the glass of wine and got up. "I think I'll walk around a bit," he announced. "Anna, you wanna come?"

"No," Anna said. "Catharine is fussy, she's getting tired. I'll stay here with her for now."

Eddie left and moved around the small group of dancers in front of the bandstand. He talked with friends as he walked around, shaking hands, and getting hugs.

Near the bandstand, he heard a familiar male voice whispering to another person. "This is the last Columbus Day celebration in the West End, eh?"

He whipped around and saw Johnny Scuro, Nero's assistant, smiling and talking with a guy he didn't know. "What the heck?" Eddie muttered under his breath. "The lousy traitor. What does this mean?"

A Roman candle suddenly shot off across the courtyard and over the harbor. Everyone stood transfixed as the sky was illumined with beautiful reds, whites, and greens, followed by a thundering boom. Eddie started back through the milling crowd to be with the tenement people. Someone pulled at his arm and turned him around—Julia.

"Hi, Eddie," she said. "Happy Columbus Day," Julia added as she reached around his neck and kissed him on the mouth.

"Jesus, you're crazy," he cried out. "My wife's sitting right over there."

"What's an old girlfriend gonna do?" Julia laughed as the rockets exploded overhead. "So, you wanna introduce me to your daughter Catharine? I've never seen her close up."

Eddie was angry. "Maybe later, Julia, maybe you should spend some time with that louse of a boyfriend you have over there. I don't know what's going on with him and you."

"Oh my God," she shouted. "You're jealous."

Eddie shook his head. "You don't get it, do you?"

Julia looked confused and suddenly angry. She turned away and stormed through the crowd.

Eddie wiped his lips and returned to the table with Anna and Catharine.

Anna took his hand and forced a smile. She had seen Julia muscle her way through in pursuit of Eddie. She dared not say a thing. Not now. But this work Eddie was doing through The Club...and now Julia Tocci.

She bit her lip, stared up at the night sky illuminated by fireworks, and clung firmly to his hand.

10

THE CHURCH

Early on the Tuesday morning following the Columbus Day celebration, Mr. Lazzaro asked Eddie to accompany him to an important meeting. He knocked on Eddie's apartment door and was greeted by Eddie himself. "Come get ready, Eddie," Mr. Lazzaro said, standing in the doorway. "A cab will be coming for us."

Anna smiled nervously. Eddie spun out of the bathroom, adjusting his tie.

"This was such short notice," he said as Anna adjusted the collar on his dress shirt. He was wearing his one and only suit, a dark blue pinstripe of very fine wool with a dark red silk tie.

"Oh," Anna said. "You look fine."

Mr. Lazzaro nodded his approval.

"Jeez, it's not every day you get to meet with the Archbishop," Eddie said. He gave Anna and Catharine a farewell kiss and went out with Mr. Lazzaro to wait on the sidewalk for the taxi.

"How did you get this meeting?" Eddie asked, still adjusting to the suit.

"Well," Mr. Lazzaro started to explain, "after the picnic, I decided to start at the top. Do something, you know? Act."

"Great," Eddie said. "Because I've been feeling so frustrated. So much talk, no action. How did you make this contact?"

Making their way down the tenement stairs, Mr. Lazzaro thought for a minute. "Let's say I have a few friends at the Chancellory. You know, over the years, I've known many priests, and well, sometimes somebody makes it to the top...or near the top."

"Ah, I see," Eddie nodded, as they stood waiting in front of the tenement. A cab pulled up. They climbed in, and Eddie heard a noise above him. Looking up, he saw Anna and Catharine waving goodbye. He saluted them and disappeared into the backseat with Mr. Lazzaro.

In a few short blocks the taxi exited the West End and merged with the heavy downtown traffic. Snaking through the skyscrapers of the financial district and the looming granite fixtures of the State buildings, they inched their way through the shadowed streets. On the far side of the downtown crush, the taxi pulled into a quiet side boulevard and entered a circular drive to an impressive, elegant marble building—the Chancellory, the headquarters of the Archbishop of Boston. Only the Archbishop of New York was more important in the United States.

They went through the heavy doors, inquired after the Archbishop's office, and were escorted down a series of corridors. They passed numerous priests, nuns, and business people hurrying past them, probably talking about complex matters of church finances and the like. Eddie strained to hear a cluster of attorneys conferring over an upcoming case. A Monsignor sighed and shook his head in frustration.

"We must do something quickly," he said to the lawyers who were popping the latches on their briefcases and scribbling notes.

Finally, they were delivered to the Archbishop's waiting room by the front desk escort, a portly gentleman, who reminded Eddie of one of the parish's sextons. The room was cavernous. Thirty or more people were seated on plush leather chairs and sofas. Potted ferns and palms broke up the waiting spaces where various petitioning groups huddled, talking quietly amongst themselves. Eddie and Mr. Lazzaro looked at each other with surprise. Mr. Lazzaro approached a secretary in the center of the room.

"Excuse me," Mr. Lazzaro said. "I believe I have an appointment with the Archbishop this morning. At ten fifteen."

"Names...?"

"Lazzaro and Sveglio."

The woman wore half glasses and smiled demurely, flipping the pages of a huge appointment book. She searched carefully and tapped a line near the bottom of the page with her fountain pen.

"Ah yes, here we are. And the purpose of your visit?" the woman asked as she stared over her glasses.

"Well," Mr. Lazzaro began to say. "We'll be talking about West End matters."

"West End matters," the woman repeated, continuing to stare at Mr. Lazzaro and Eddie for a second. Eddie felt a chill run down his spine.

"Well, certainly," she said. "Please take a seat. We'll call you when there's an opportunity."

"An opportunity?" Mr. Lazzaro exclaimed. "I have an appointment at ten-fifteen."

"Oh, that's a general reporting time. Once here, the Archbishop and his staff handle meetings as time permits. Please, take a seat. We'll call you, sir."

They took a seat in the deep chairs and began to read the newspaper. They waited and waited. Ten fifteen passed, eleven and twelve came and went. Mr. Lazzaro approached the receptionist's desk several times. Each time he returned with a shrug. He and Eddie made small talk, but Eddie could see Mr. Lazzaro was increasingly disheartened.

"Hey, it's okay," Eddie said, trying to reassure Mr. Lazzaro. "We can come back another day. You know how much red tape there is when it comes to the Church."

"Yes, but I spoke with a very important bishop to get this appointment. I frankly thought he had more pull. I'm quite surprised. Disappointed is more like it."

"Who knows? We may still get called any minute," Eddie offered.

"I guess there are a lot of problems facing the Church," Mr. Lazzaro said.

"Yeah, like making a buck," Eddie said, as he remembered the lawyers and the Monsignor down the hall. The place smelled like a plush courthouse with crucifixes. Eddie dozed off briefly as the clock rang soft, but rich, the single note of one in the afternoon.

Suddenly, Eddie felt someone tugging at his sleeve.

"Come on," Mr. Lazzaro said, "We've been called at last. Now we'll throw some fire back at the Mayor and his plans for the West End."

"Fire from above?" Eddie asked as they were led through two offices and then a maze of corridors. An ornate, legal reference room was their final destination. A priest and a man in a business suit met them. Eddie missed their names. It was not the Archbishop. It was some priest who was a lawyer and another lawyer who was not a priest. Mr. Lazzaro spoke quietly and briefly in Italian, in hushed tones.

Then the discussion broke into English and yammered on for several minutes in legalese concerning the federal grants, administrative law, the Church's official position, the years of maneuvering—Mr. Lazzaro and Eddie were swallowed by the details.

"What you're saying," Mr. Lazzaro said at last, "...what you're saying is there's nothing you can do now. You have saved the school and Holy Name Church and its grounds, and that's enough for the Church? Is this right?"

"Basically, although with easements," the priest went on sounding like a real estate expert.

"But what about the people of the West End?" Mr. Lazzaro asked. "What good will that do you if the community moves away?"

Handing Mr. Lazzaro a weighty document, the priest continued. "Ah, well of course, people will return," the priest assured him. "A fairly large percentage of the rebuilding will include residential sections. This study, recently completed by the Urban Planning Department at Harvard--a study authored in part by a former resident of the West End, Joseph Angelino—I believe points to the opportunity for a return migration of former residents once rebuilding occurs."

"But it may not include residential housing that is within the means of us who live there now," Mr. Lazzaro protested. "I came here to meet with the Archbishop today, but instead, I hear you talk about the Church being pleased with its settlement."

"You've sold out to the City, right?" Eddie grumbled. Mr. Lazzaro tugged at Eddie's sleeve in restraint. Joe Angelino would be on his hit list for sure now, Eddie thought.

Mr. Lazzaro and Eddie looked at each other and shrugged. "I'm afraid that's all the time we have today, gentlemen," the priest said. "You're welcome to read the various studies that have been done. That may convince you that it will not be as bad as it might seem. Really, the Church has always been concerned with improving the neighborhood conditions of its parishioners. Frankly, the West End is long overdue."

Before they knew it, Eddie and Mr. Lazzaro were back in a cab returning to the West End. Mr. Lazzaro passed the urban planning study to Eddie, who rolled it into a tight cylinder. They exchanged few words on the return ride home. As they parted at the top of the stairs, Eddie wanted to explode with anger.

"I'm sorry, Eddie," Mr. Lazzaro said.

"Wait until I see Father Mora at Holy Name this Sunday," Eddie said. "I'm gonna send a message to the Archbishop through him."

"Calm down, Eddie. Father Mora can't do a thing at his level, really. You see how it is."

"We have to get tough, Mr. Lazzaro. They won't listen until something big happens."

"Well, there are other ways. I have a few more ideas," Mr. Lazzaro said, brightening. "Yes, there are quite a few more strings to pull. Let's get together later and do some planning Eddie, what do you say?"

"Fine, I'm ready anytime you are."

The following Saturday, prior to the Women's March on City Hall, the women of the neighborhood met at various homes to plan their march. Anna attended one of the meetings to help make signs. On Sunday morning, Eddie, Anna, and Catharine got ready for Mass.

That same morning across the landing, Mr. Lazzaro awakened with sunlight warming him through his bedroom window. In the distance, he could hear the parish church bells. He dressed and ate a little breakfast, and then, as was his weekly custom, he sat in his rocking chair waiting for Eddie and Anna to stop by to walk to church with him.

He picked up his wife's photo which sat on the table nearby. Suddenly he had an urge to open their old keepsake memory chest. He went through her photos and souvenirs tenderly. He discovered a gold butterfly brooch wrapped in white cloth that brought back a rush of memory. He picked up a photo album, and the brooch, and returned to his rocker.

He leafed through the old black and white photographs. He studied a photo of himself and Catharine, taken when they were young and newly married in Italy. In one photograph he held the reins of a horse. He and Catharine were sitting side by side in a wagon loaded with the old chest.

In his daydream, the moment was clear, as though it had happened only yesterday. His brother-in-law, Geraldo, was still a young man and he stood there in the road with the camera, snapping their picture. Near the road behind him were relatives and friends from the village.

"I'll send this to you in America," Geraldo promised.

Maria, Geraldo's wife, and sister to Catharine, handed Catharine the gold butterfly brooch.

"Here," Maria said with tears in her eyes. "I want you to have this. It may bring you good luck."

"We better get going," Geraldo said, as he climbed into the wagon. Family and friends hugged them and clustered about the wagon one last time. Mr. Lazzaro's heart was aching as the horses set out smartly for the train station.

"I wish you were coming along with us," Mr. Lazzaro said to Geraldo, throwing an arm around him.

"Maybe someday, maybe someday," Geraldo said, his voice cracking.

Tears fell from Mr. Lazzaro's eyes. He knew in his heart he might never see them again. He puffed out his chest and pointed to the fields defiantly.

"Let the landowners work their own fields!" he proclaimed. He hugged Catharine. "Catharine and I, we're going to America to start our new life."

A gentle knocking at the door brought Mr. Lazzaro out of his daydream. It was Anna calling him to church. He put down the album and tucked the butterfly brooch into his coat pocket. Walking down the stairwell together, they saw in the foyer two nuns dragging Nunzio and another boy off to church. They followed the nuns down the street with other parishioners on their way to the 11 AM Mass.

They joined other tenement residents and sat in a pew near the front of the Holy Name Church. Its medieval buttresses swept over them with its weight of tradition. The voice of Father Mora echoed throughout the hollows and alcoves of the beautiful old church. Many parishioners had been baptized there, and many more had passed on through the side door to the adjoining cemetery.

During the mass, Mr. Lazzaro seemed dreamy and quiet. Eddie watched him with curiosity. He felt badly about the way Mr. Lazzaro had been treated on Friday at the Chancellory.

Prior to the benediction, Father Mora stepped to the podium. "Before you leave I have an announcement to make," he said, staring up at the lofty, dim roof beam. "Like all of you, I am deeply saddened by the City's decision to redevelop this area. My sympathy lies with you."

Eddie and Mr. Lazzaro looked at each other with surprise.

"However, we must all make plans for the future," Father Mora went on to say. "I am sorry to announce that the parish school will not accept new students next September, and at the end of the next school year the parish school will be closed."

There was a groan of disappointment.

"That's not what they said Friday," Eddie whispered to Mr. Lazzaro.

Mr. Lazzaro patted his arm and shook his head resignedly. Eddie was seeing red.

The priest went on. "I know many of you bitterly disagree with the Archbishop's decision to support redevelopment of the West End. However, let me assure you that he has your best interests in mind."

Father Mora suddenly threw out his arms. "At least we know this church will be spared. After you have left the West End and are settled in your new homes and apartments, I hope you will return to visit us. Our doors will always be open. Please rise and bow your heads for God's blessing."

With the end of the service, they filed out the front of the church. Eddie lined up to speak with Father Mora. He wanted to go on record with how he felt. Anna and Catharine took a seat on the church steps, while Mr. Lazzaro turned and walked out into the cemetery.

He stood over his wife's tombstone. His own name was engraved next to hers with only his birth date. She had died so suddenly from a cerebral hemorrhage, such an unlikely occurrence for a woman so young. The Second World War had just begun. He couldn't believe how quickly she had left him. It seemed like a long time ago, but then some days, it felt as though it happened only yesterday—especially lately.

He knelt down and prayed for her soul while holding the brooch in his hands. He spoke aloud to her in Italian. "Catharine. I found this from a long time ago," he said quietly. "It was with so many memories of you in the chest at home. Please forgive me if I have not always done the best for you, my love. I wish you could be here now. I need your help."

He stood in silence for a minute, and then his eyes were pulled as if by an invisible force toward two other graves nearby. He walked slowly over to them. They were the gravestones of Eddie's father and mother. Eddie's father's tombstone was decrepit--looking now; he had died in the war. But Rosa, Eddie's mother, her grave was only a few years old. He remembered the day they had walked here together, sharing their mutual grief. Her husband had been killed in the war during the invasion at Normandy. Then came the death of his own wife within a day or two. Rosa had, despite her own grief, come to the funeral for Catharine. Rosa and he shared their grief and gave comfort to one another. Throughout the years, she had allowed him to become a father figure for Eddie.

He prayed silently for Rosa, for her husband, and for Catharine. *What a world we live in,* he thought to himself.

Startled by Eddie suddenly standing there beside him, Mr. Lazzaro got up from his knees. He saw that Eddie's face was flushed with anger. Anna stood close behind him holding Catharine.

"I can't get anywhere with Father Mora. This is no joke. This is not just a scare," Eddie ranted.

"Father Mora talked like this is going to happen. There's no turning back," Anna said.

"The Church just doesn't care," Eddie blurted out.

Mr. Lazzaro took the butterfly brooch from his pocket and came over to Anna. "Here," he offered. "I want little Catharine to have this. It belonged to my wife."

"Oh no," Anna said. "How nice, Mr. Lazzaro. But we couldn't." Anna looked at Eddie for help. He shrugged in confusion.

"Please," Mr. Lazzaro insisted. "Won't you humor an old man and his memories? Please..." He pinned the brooch to Catharine's collar.

They started walking home. Mr. Lazzaro was pensive and withdrawn. Eddie tried to engage him in conversation about the West End's future. Eddie pointed to the façade of the tenement as they stood on the sidewalk.

"This home is the only home I've ever had," Eddie said. "I'm going to do all I can to save it."

"Of course," Mr. Lazzaro agreed.

Eddie, his face flushed with emotion, pressed on. "When I was growing up I had this as a home. These people and all the memories. This is my home...forever. Maybe other people don't care about where they were born, but for me and lots of others here in the West End, it still matters."

"Of course it does," Mr. Lazzaro said. "Don't worry, Eddie, we're only beginning to fight City Hall."

"And don't forget the Mothers' March," Anna reminded them, starting up the tenement steps with Catharine. "That's something we'll be doing tomorrow. Come on you two, let's have a nice dinner. I made beef braciole. Should be nice and tender. It's been cooking in the gravy since seven this morning."

Mr. Lazzaro and Eddie smiled at each other. "What would we do without the women?" Eddie asked. "This West End army runs on its stomach!"

11

THE WOMEN'S PROTEST

On Monday morning at ten-thirty, only a handful of women and children were congregated in front of the State House near the Boston Common. Anna, Catharine in her buggy, Anna's mother, and a number of other neighborhood women waited patiently for more supporters to come. Bill Warren, their volunteer community organizer, sat on a park bench and waited with them.

Finally, he pulled them together and announced. "Ladies, I appreciate all of you coming here today. It's now almost eleven. I hoped there would be a larger turnout. I'm afraid our group is much too small to be effective. I think we'd better cancel the march and return home."

Anna stood up. "Well, I don't know what happened to all the others, but we do have this petition, Mr. Warren...a lot of people have signed it. And I called a *Globe* reporter and told them about this march."

"Oh, you did," Warren said. "That was good thinking. But as you can see, even the reporter didn't show."

"Yes but..." Anna tried to continue.

"I think too many people are not taking the City seriously enough, perhaps that's why they're not here. Though this has been going on for years, the Mayor's political machine will be hard to stop this time. I sure hope there will be a bigger response at our community meeting this week." Warren said.

"Mr. Warren," Anna spoke out. "I think we should at least march over to City Hall."

There was a small chorus of approval and several women shook their protest signs. "Wipe Out Crime, Not People," one sign read.

"Well, why not?" Mr. Warren agreed. "Okay, let's head out."

The women's brigade made its way along the narrow streets between the State House and Government Center, where City Hall overlooked the harbor. A few state politicos stopped momentarily to take in the small band's protest message, then went on with their business. When the group arrived on the steps of City Hall, a young woman came running toward them.

"Oh, hi," she said, gasping. "I'm Cindy White from the *Boston Globe*. My editor said to meet you here at City Hall."

"We started at the State House," Anna said with a smile. "Thanks for coming."

"Is this it?" Cindy asked, looking around at the hearty little group.

"I'm afraid we've had a problem getting the numbers we wanted for this walk. It may be West End's residents don't realize the seriousness of the urban renewal."

"Excuse me," Cindy said. "But who are you, sir?"

Mr. Warren went on to explain his role while Cindy scribbled in her notebook.

"So, in other words, this is it for today?" Cindy questioned.

Mrs. Petrini, one of the long-term residents of the West End, pushed her way forward. "I think—well, we're here. Let's talk with the Mayor."

Mr. Warren laughed and shook his head in agreement.

"Why not," Mrs. Petrini went on. "You see, we have our reporter here. We have our petition. Our babies and mothers. What more do we need to talk with the Mayor? I say we go through the doors and demand to see the Mayor!"

"Yeah, let's try," the women said.

Everyone looked at Mr. Warren who smiled indulgently and shrugged. "Why not?" he asked. "What can we lose?"

Accompanied by their reporter and Mr. Warren, the small band of women and children swept through the big doors and arrived at the information desk, their requests to see the Mayor echoing inside the cavernous marble foyer. There were the usual phone calls and hurrying of minor officials, faces appearing over balconies, but news that a *Globe* reporter was downstairs with an irate small army of West End mothers got action. In ten minutes, they were in the Mayor's outer office. In fifteen minutes, the Mayor had interrupted "an important budget conference with top advisors," as one flunky put it, ushering the protestors into a long meeting room. In the center of the table was the model of the West End development.

Mayor Cowley rolled into the room in his wheelchair. He was smiling and nodding. "I want to thank you for coming to make your concerns known," he said. "I understand you have a petition."

Mr. Warren took the roll of names from Anna's mother and handed it to the Mayor, who examined it briefly.

"Well," the Mayor said, clearing his throat for a speech. "It's certainly part of our open door policy to the neighborhoods to hear the complaints of ordinary citizens. That's what makes a city like Boston such a nice place to live in. We take the time to listen, to engage in dialogue with concerned groups. I want to thank you for this input, and I want to state again that we are entirely sympathetic with your worries about this transition that is going to take place in an important community in our fine city."

"So what can you do, Mr. Mayor?" Mrs. Petrini asked. "Can you call this whole thing off?"

"Ahh..." the Mayor hesitated. He finally began to take notice that the women were real and could speak. "Yes, we can do many things, in this office. And I want you to know that we have made every effort to make this a sane and rational process. We will have a complete transition team of urban planners, housing specialists, and community outreach workers available throughout the transformation. We told the Federal Government from the start, we said, 'You gotta give us money to compensate for the people's difficulties with the transition.' We said that, yes we did."

The women looked at each other as the Mayor glanced over the names again.

"Well," he said. "I must get back to this taxation conference. We're under a deadline that won't go away. Again, thank you, ladies and gentleman," the Mayor said, nodding and squinting at Mr. Warren. "Your feedback will be incorporated in our, ah, decision making process. Thank you." His aide wheeled him expertly from the room, leaving the marchers alone.

When they returned home, Anna put Catharine down for a nap. Eddie sat with her in the living room and heard the sad tale of their weak showing.

"Hey, at least you pushed your way into the Mayor's Office. Sounds like that guy Warren might be a quitter."

"Oh, I don't know," Anna said.

"And the rest of the women in the neighborhood too. Where were they? Quitters!" Eddie said with rising anger.

"Maybe we didn't advertise the march enough," Anna realized.

"Forget it, Anna. The problem is people don't think this is for real. They think someone will save them, save their lives here."

"Maybe some people don't care as much about the West End as we do. Maybe some people are ready to move out and start a new life," Anna figured.

Eddie studied her closely. "Then they're stupid. They don't appreciate what they have here. They're fools."

Anna flushed slightly.

"And notice what the Mayor said to you, Anna," Eddie pointed out. "He kept talking about the transition team, the outreach workers, and all that bull. You know who's sucking off that payroll, don't you?"

"Who?" Anna asked.

"That traitor, Joe Angelino! That's who!" Eddie shouted.

"Oh, Eddie, he can't be the whole problem," Anna replied, trying to calm him.

"Of course not," Eddie said. "But everywhere we go we keep running into that guy. He's come back to haunt us. "

Anna frowned.

"And where was Jenny?" Eddie asked. "She's a cousin of Angel's. Was she there today?"

"No, and she had promised she would be," Anna said.

Eddie was already on his feet and headed for the door.

"Where are you going?" Anna asked.

"War has to start on the home front," Eddie declared, smiling, "and you have to start by rooting out the traitors and spies right under your own roof."

"Oh, Eddie," Anna cried. "Please don't start any trouble."

"Who? Me?" he said with a glare, disappearing down the stairs. In several bounds, he was in front of Jenny and her husband Tony 's apartment door. He knocked and waited impatiently.

Jenny was about Eddie's age. She was thin and soft-spoken. She peeked out the door and smiled wanly at Eddie.

"Hi Jenny. What happened at the march today?"

"Oh, hi Eddie," she said softly. "How are you?"

"Oh, I'm okay, Jenny. Just great. How'd the march go? You did go, didn't you?"

"Not exactly," Jenny answered timidly.

"Why not?" asked Eddie, leaning down to look in her sad eyes.

"Well, I didn't go actually. Tony wouldn't let me. Said he didn't want me to make a public display of myself. He called it a circus."

"Jesus," Eddie exclaimed. "Has Tony gone crazy?"

"I don't know. Sometimes I just don't understand him," she whispered and stepped out of the door.

"Doesn't sound like Tony to me. Sounds like your cousin Angel has been getting to you both. That's what it sounds like to me, Jenny," Eddie implied.

"No, Eddie, it's not Angel's doing. No..."

"Yeah, right! So you mean Tony didn't realize how important this march was?"

"Well, you know Tony," Jenny answered. "He has some funny ways about him. He won't believe it's going to happen until he sees something torn down."

"Oh, that's just great, just great!" Eddie said with disgust. "Is Tony in there now?"

"Ahh..." Jenny hesitated.

"Who's out there?" called Tony, hearing the commotion and coming to the door.

"I wanna talk with you. Step out here," Eddie demanded.

"What the heck is going on?" Tony yelled.

"You've got no guts Tony!" Eddie shouted back. "You're siding with the enemy."

"What is this?" Tony asked, looking confused and glancing at Jenny.

"Don't play stupid!" Eddie stated. "You're listening to Joe Angelino. You told your wife not to march against City Hall to save the West End. You're turning on us, you're folding."

"You're full of hot air," Tony said laughing. He shook his head.

"Admit it," Eddie pressed. "You're selling out."

"I don't have to take this crap!" Tony responded.

Eddie gave him a shove in his shoulder. "You want to leave? Why don't you start now?" Eddie said, giving him another shove toward the foyer door.

Anna yelled down the stairwell.

"Eddie, that's enough!"

Eddie swallowed hard and stepped back. Tenement residents were gathering on the landings up the stairwell, watching the action.

"Yeah, that's enough," Tony said, laughing again. He stepped up to Eddie and got right in his face. "You know, you're way outta line. You don't know who your friends are, do you?"

"Don't push me, Tony," Eddie warned.

"Accept the fact, Eddie," Tony retorted. "You guys can't stop this one. The West End is history!"

Tony shoved Eddie away from his door. Eddie stepped forward in one movement and caught Tony under the chin with a hard right hook that lifted him off his feet. Tony fell to the foyer floor and collapsed. Jenny screamed and rushed to his aid. Anna shouted and practically flew down the stairs.

Hearing the shouting, Mr. Lazzaro had emerged from his apartment and was frowning down at the bedlam. Tony shook his head a couple of times and tried to focus on Eddie.

"Man, you're cracking up," Tony mumbled. His jaw was starting to swell. Jenny was crying.

Anna hovered over Tony and, looking up, shot a fierce glance at Eddie.

"Eddie," she said with tears in her eyes. "Go back upstairs! Now!"

Eddie shook his head in disgust and marched out of the foyer, slamming the doors behind him.

12

COMMUNITY MEETING

In mid-March on a Wednesday morning, West End residents saw a City vehicle moving a trailer office onto an empty lot near the Holy Name School yard. They put up a wooden sign proclaiming the spot as the headquarters for the "West End Redevelopment—Communities in Cooperation."

Joe Angelino and his small staff arrived around midday. Eddie heard about it and went for a look. A cop was idling around the property and keeping a close watch on the passersby.

Eddie stood on the street and stared at the windows of the trailer. A secretary inside noticed him; then Angel also looked out the window. He went to the door and called out to Eddie.

"Come in, let's talk!"

"There's nothing to talk about!" Eddie shouted back. "You've come here to ruin us."

The cop stood up from his folding chair and walked to the corner of the trailer.

"So, you have to have police protection," Eddie said. "You must be doing the right thing."

"Ah come on, relax Eddie," Angel said, stepping out of the trailer and starting toward him. The cop came to attention, watching closely.

Eddie turned and walked away, shaking his head. Angel stopped and threw up his arms in resignation.

That evening, Eddie and Mr. Lazzaro walked over to the school auditorium for a community meeting, which had been called in response to the unwelcome presence of the City's new site office within their community. Mr. Lazzaro had been one of the meeting's organizers. He'd talked on the phone to several people and had a plan to propose. Along the way to the meeting, Mr. Lazzaro and Eddie passed the redevelopment trailer. They noticed the lights were still on.

"That Angel," Mr. Lazzaro said. "He was always a hard worker. We got our work cut out for us."

"Angel doesn't have any idea how angry this community is," Eddie said. "If he thinks, because he got this important job, he can wave his Federal Guidelines and we'll jump through his hoops, he's got another thing coming."

Upon their arrival at the auditorium, they were pleased to see a large crowd had gathered. Seated on the stage were Bill Warren, Representative Nero, and John Lanington, a former Redevelopment Commissioner. Lanington had resigned the previous year in protest over the strong-arm tactics of the Mayor's office. Joining them was Josh Cohen who ran the leading West End meat market. He was there to represent his own business interests, as well as those of other shop owners. Mr. Lazzaro climbed the stairs to the stage and sat down with a wave at many friends in the audience. Nero took the podium first.

"I want to tell you about George Benson, the contractor who wants to demolish this area," Nero said. "Did you know that George Benson is the Mayor's right hand man?"

The crowd booed.

"That he helped the Mayor get elected? Did you also know that two days before the Mayor awarded the contract—just two days—Mr. Benson went out and formed a corporation? Did you know that his corporation only had a thousand dollars in equity at the time? That's illegal!" Nero shouted. The crowd booed again.

Leaning forward excitingly, Nero said, "he should have had at least a hundred thousand dollar bond!" And to top it all off, Mr. Benson was only the second lowest bidder. Don't you think that sounds a little fishy?"

The crowd booed again. Excited conversations and general agitation stirred in the hall.

"Guess the Mayor wanted to keep it in the family," Nero went on to say. "The Mayor is first and foremost a politician. He acts like he's some kind of Russian czar! I'm telling you, the Mayor is a legal racketeer! We've got to deal with this Mayor."

Eddie, from his front row seat, heard someone shout, "Yeah, the only way we're going to accomplish anything is for us to go down to City Hall...and not send our wives!"

Another man jumped from his seat and yelled, "Let's go down there and drag the bum and his gang out of their offices!"

Eddie turned and saw a third man he didn't recognize shouting, "Let's have a hundred car caravan and drive down to City Hall!"

The crowd became increasingly unruly. Nero tried to calm them, but failed. Finally, Josh Cohen went to the podium.

"Wait a minute. Hold on. I'm just as angry as all of you. My father and I will lose the meat market."

A man in the back cried out, "Sit down!"

"No, not until you listen to me," Josh insisted, while adjusting the microphone. He held up a book. "See this? It says that under state law the City cannot charge rents in areas taken by eminent domain. I've thought of a plan we all can follow. I think this way we can persuade the Mayor and his machine."

Several men groaned in protest.

"Now listen," Josh said. "First of all, don't pay rent to the City since it has broken the law. Secondly, don't move out of your homes. Thirdly, let's have a peaceful march to the Mayor's office and present him with a plan for rehabilitating the area with our rent money."

A man spoke up loudly. "This area doesn't need rehabilitation!"

Another shouted, "This place ain't no slum! You sound like the BRA."

Eddie looked out at the crowd and thought he recognized the speaker—a guy from The Club, and he was making perfect sense.

Another angry resident shouted, "Let's go to City Hall and bust the Mayor's door down. That's the only language he'll understand!"

Josh quieted the crowd. "Look, we must persuade the Mayor with nonviolent methods."

Someone shouted, "Will you sit down?"

Another yelled, "Let us do things our way. Sit down before we sit you down!"

Eddie looked at this man. The face was familiar, but he didn't know him personally. Mario might know him. Where was Mario? He wondered. Then he remembered his friend had gone on another errand for Buddy. Another driving errand.

The crowd became even more rowdy. Two of the tough guys started toward the podium. Eddie beat them to it and reached the microphone.

"Hey, not now! Listen a minute! You guys sit down." I think Josh has got some good ideas. He's telling you not to give your rents to the City until it fixes up the area for us, whatever it is that they think needs fixin'. It's good news to me to learn the City can't collect our rent legally. I think we should give his method a try."

A tall, Brahmin-like figure in a bow tie walked over to Eddie and whispered to him. Eddie relinquished the podium and sat down next to Mr. Lazzaro who patted him approvingly on the shoulder.

"I'm John Lanington. The Federal Government appointed me to be on the redevelopment commission. Because of these shenanigans down at City Hall, I resigned last year. During the past few weeks, I've looked over your neighborhood and I agree with you; It's a neighborhood, not a slum."

There were cries of approval.

"In fact, I think the BRA exaggerated the blight of the West End in order to obtain federal funding. This area does not warrant demolition but could use some improvements."

Now came boos and catcalls.

Lanington pressed on. "I know you don't like hearing that, but I'm talking about things like widening the streets so fire trucks can pass through. And some of those vacant buildings in the area could be knocked down and replaced with playground facilities. I want you to know I plan to talk to the authorities about this neighborhood. I'll present them with my suggestions. I'm not saying I can guarantee anything, but I'll try to speak as a liaison on your behalf."

The crowd applauded enthusiastically. Mr. Lazzaro went to the podium and looked over a few scraps of paper he pulled from his suit jacket.

"Now, finally, let an old man from the West End, a man who came here from Italy in his youth, let me tell you I think we have all forgotten that we have the resource of the law behind us. My old friend Philip Mazzei, the esteemed attorney here in Boston, has offered his services to our committee—free of charge. Unfortunately, he came down with a touch of the flu this week and cannot be here tonight. But he will be reviewing the evidence—the kind of things Josh and others have said tonight—and, well, from there I think he will try for an injunction against this whole mess the Mayor has dumped on us. I will keep you informed," Mr. Lazzaro said.

Shortly thereafter the meeting broke up.

Josh shook Eddie's hand. "Thanks for your support."

"What you said sounded good to me," Eddie said. "Mr. Lazzaro's idea too."

"I've always felt a part of this community, even though my family doesn't live here anymore," Josh said. "My father has really been upset about the prospect of losing the market. This was his retirement security."

"The same goes for lots of the elderly," Mr. Lazzaro said.

John Lanington approached Eddie and Josh.

"I was very impressed by both of you and your protest," he said smiling.

"Do you think we have a chance with the BRA?" Josh asked.

"I honestly don't know," Lanington said. "I don't know how the City could target this area, calling it deteriorated, a slum. I'm also concerned about what Representative Nero had to say about the Mayor and the developer."

"Yes, it doesn't sound right. I think that could tie in with Mr. Lazzaro's attorney, Mr. Mazei?"

Eddie asked Lanington, "When do you plan to talk with the Mayor?"

"Maybe sometime next week," Lanington replied. "If he'll still talk to me."

"Can you drop by our new Storefront Office to let us know what happens? I forgot to mention tonight that a few of us are setting up a space in the old furniture store." It's right across the street from the BRA's trailer. We're right in their face!" Josh laughed.

"Sure. I'll call to let you know when I'll be by," Lanington said, searching his pockets. "What's your number?"

Josh said, "Here, I'll write it down for you." Then, turning to Eddie, he said, "I hope you'll be stopping by. We need your support."

"Beautiful, just beautiful," Eddie agreed. "You can bet I'll be down."

Shortly thereafter, Eddie and Mr. Lazzaro left the auditorium and began the walk home together.

"It was quite a night, eh?" Mr. Lazzaro said.

"I was impressed," Eddie admitted. "Maybe we have a shot."

They noticed the lights were out in Angel's trailer, and stopped across the street. They stared into the empty furniture store window where the West End opposition would be lodged. Then they strolled on down to the tenement.

"Don't worry, Eddie," Mr. Lazzaro said as they parted in the hallway.

"I thought you were the great worrier," Eddie laughed. "I always looked up to you as a worrier."

Mr. Lazzaro smiled. "Do as I say, not as I do. You want to live a long life? Then don't worry. Anyway, everything works out for the best."

"Okay, I'll sleep on that," Eddie replied. "I'm gonna tell Anna about the meeting. Until tomorrow..."

"Tomorrow. Good night," Mr. Lazzaro said, watching Eddie disappear behind his apartment door.

13

THE JUDGE

It wasn't until April, on a Tuesday after Patriot's Day, that Mr. Lazzaro, Eddie, and others from the West End had the opportunity to have a hearing before a judge. Representing the West End families was attorney Philip Mazzei, a very proud Italian, whose blood line went back to the American Revolution. It had been his ancestor, Dr. Filippo Mazzei, friend of Benjamin Franklin and Thomas Jefferson, and activist writer during the revolution, who wrote in a pamphlet "all men are by nature equally free and independent," from which the founding fathers coined "all men are created equal.

Philip Mazzei wore his family's history as a badge of honor proudly. He felt a responsibility and duty to seek justice for the families of the old West End. Like Mr. Lazzaro, he was first generation Italian-American. Despite repeated frustrations blocking his career on the Boston legal scene, dominated by long-established W.A.S.P. law firms, he had risen in the ranks of practicing attorneys. Now in his seventies and semi-retired from his partnership, his keen legal mind continued to dispel doubts about his competence.

Mr. Lazzaro regaled Eddie and Josh with several stories as they drove over to the Federal Building. Philip Mazei had requested a review of development plans for the purpose of exposing certain undeniable legal conflicts. What he hoped to do was get an injunction delaying further development until the politics behind the scenes destroyed its forward momentum.

Within the lofty marble halls of the courthouse with its open stairwells and circular staircases milled the crowds of petitioners, plaintiffs, defendants, bailiffs, police, witnesses, and attorneys. They were all seeking justice.

The West End group assembled in the main concourse. Some twenty or more concerned West End residents joined Mr. Lazzaro, Eddie, and Josh. Mr. Mazzei, looking diminutive but natty in his neatly pressed Brooks Brothers suit, pulled the group to the side of the hallway.

"My friends, this is merely a hearing," Mr. Mazzei explained. "We will demonstrate a few obvious violations of the development code."

"Like the City cannot collect rents?" Eddie complained.

"Yes, that's one issue. As I have explained to my good friend Joseph," the attorney said, nodding toward Mr. Lazzaro, "I am not a specialist in this area, but the law is fairly clear. There is a lot of administrative law connected with the BRA and there are a lot of housing issues in general. Still, I am hopeful we will at least get a full hearing for an injunction."

"Great!" Eddie replied hopefully.

"Well," Mr. Mazzei said, "let's find our courtroom. It certainly never hurts to show good neighborhood support."

They followed the attorney down a corridor, who led the way with his arthritic limp. He carried a battered leather briefcase that slapped against his leg as he mounted a wide staircase. At the top of the stairs, a bailiff pointed to their courtroom. They filed into the somber room with its old, tall windows covered in grime.

Mr. Mazzei pointed out seats behind the plaintiff's table. The City's attorneys showed up soon after the West Enders were settled in. A young attorney with a crew cut and broad grin approached Mr. Mazzei and introduced himself.

"Hi, I'm Sam Ellison with the City's legal office. Just thought I'd say hello," he said, shaking Mr. Mazzei's hand and nodding to the West End group. "I've been an admirer of your legal work. I once wrote a brief in law school drawing on your tariff cases."

"Ah, yes," Mr. Mazzei said and smiled. "Well, thank you for the compliment."

"I just want you to know, ah, no matter how this turns out, I'm a big fan of yours. Nice meeting you," Ellison said. He seemed to hesitate before saying more. "Well, nice meeting you," he said again and returned to his table with his assistants.

Mr. Mazzei sat down and leaned back to confer with Mr. Lazzaro, Eddie, and Josh.

"That was very solicitous," Mazzei whispered. "You don't often have the City acting quite so nice. Not like the old days. Who knows? Maybe things are changing downtown."

The group looked at him skeptically.

"Yes, my sentiments exactly," Mr. Mazzei said, laughing softly.

"All rise," the bailiff announced and the honorable Gerald T. McSwain, heavy-jowled judge of the appellant court, swept into the room. He gathered his black robes about him as he settled into his accustomed perch. He put on his reading glasses, looked over his paperwork, and pursed his lips. There was silence as he continued reading and flipping pages. At length he removed his glasses and stared down at the West End contingent.

The judge cleared his throat and took a sip of water.

"This is a preliminary hearing for the purpose of determining a full hearing for injunction against the BRA's redevelopment plans for the West End. I have read Mr. Mazzei's brief. Has the City had a chance to study this material?" The judge stared at the young attorney.

"Yes we have, your Honor," Mr. Ellison said, coming to his feet.

"And what is the City's position?" the judge asked, his eyes blinking like a sleepy owl.

"Your Honor," Mr. Ellison answered. "On all counts we contend the City, State, and Federal agencies have exhausted an incredible amount of labor over the years. Shall I cite the agency case materials?"

"No," the judge said with a scowl on his face.

"Then, your Honor," Mr. Ellison said, "based on the extensive hearing materials and all relevant code and agency law, we find no basis for a hearing or appeal for hearing."

The judge shook his head and looked over at Mr. Mazzei, who got to his feet slowly.

"Your Honor," Mr. Mazzei began, "I—"

"Excuse me," the judge said. "Have you anything specific adding to these matters?"

"Well, as your Honor can see," Mr. Mazzei said, walking toward the judge's bench. "There is clearly the matter of code violations as, for example, in—"

"Please," the judge said again. "I asked you, do you have anything new? This rent collection issue was waived long ago in previous hearings. I suggest, Counselor, with all due respect, you take a close look at this material. We have a whole basement full of the stuff!"

The judge chuckled and the bailiffs and City attorneys laughed along with him.

"Your Honor," Mr. Mazzei said. "We have reason to believe there are certain irregularities in the way the BRA is implementing its contracts with the City. The City, for example, has no right to collect rents."

"Mr. Mazzei," the judge admonished. "If you have nothing new for the record, I'll rule."

Mr. Mazzei, standing by his table, was dumbstruck. His fingertips tapped against the desk nervously. He looked at Mr. Ellison who looked down at his papers to avoid eye contact.

"In this request for a full hearing for the purpose of an injunction against the BRA and the West End project," the judge said rapidly, pausing and surveying the West Enders gathered in the front rows. "I find no substantive evidence for such a hearing. Case dismissed. Next case."

The people from the West End booed. The judge slammed his gavel down.

"This is a court of law!" the judge shouted. "Save your protests for the streets. Next case!"

Eddie stood up and glared at the judge, who returned the look.

"This is a railroad job," Eddie said. "The City's politicians have bought everybody off."

"I'll put you in contempt, young man," the judge shouted, his face glaring red. "Don't you insult this court, Sir!"

The bailiffs moved down front toward the group.

"Come on, Eddie," Mr. Lazzaro pleaded. He grabbed Eddie by the arm and pulled him down the aisle. Mr. Mazzei followed behind. In the hallway, the West End group argued and complained about the injustice. Mr. Mazzei was perplexed.

"Clearly," he said, trying to comfort Mr. Lazzaro and the others, "we face an uphill battle. The City has covered its tracks very well. Legally, there may be no other options. You could, of course, hire a big firm to go after them. But that takes a lot of money and then you may not gain much. Maybe not even a delay."

"What should we do then?" Mr. Petrini, the flower shop owner asked.

"Well, if they want to play hard ball, we will play even harder ball," Eddie said.

"Yes, Eddie's right," Mr. Lazzaro agreed. "I just don't understand why we're being blocked everywhere we turn."

He looked at the group of friends and sighed.

"Maybe we should meet at the Storefront Office and see what we can cook up."

"Sounds good to me," replied Josh.

"We've got to do more than plan," Eddie told them. "We've got to act."

"Be careful," Mr. Mazzei advised as they started down the staircase. "Any direct violations can put you at legal risk."

"What have we got to lose at this point?" Eddie replied.

Mr. Mazzei looked at Mr. Lazzaro and Eddie standing together and shook his head in sympathy.

"Yes," the old lawyer said. "I see your dilemma. The City's quite serious this time."

That same afternoon, the Storefront Committee, as they'd dubbed themselves, got very serious about setting up its office. Desks were brought in with supplies donated by the shops in the neighborhood. Josh and his father hauled a coffee machine and several pounds of freshly ground coffee through the front door. Money donations came in spontaneously.

Nunzio brought in a group of children who donated jars of coins they had salvaged from the streets and sidewalks. A phone truck arrived to install a phone. Eddie and Mario found several creaking office chairs in the basement and fixed them up.

Across the street, Angel and his staff watched the people coming and going into the store. The windows now proclaimed: "STOP THE MAYOR AND THE BRA! SAVE THE WEST END TODAY!"

"They're wasting their time," one of Angel's assistants said, looking at a crowd of people churning on the sidewalk across the street.

"Don't underestimate these people," Angel warned. "They just need to understand how to change with the times. A lot of the old-timers still have one foot in Italy."

"You think we can really convince them this is it?" one assistant inquired.

"We have to, even if we have to drag them kicking and screaming. This is healthy," Angel said, pointing to the sidewalk group now hoisting protest signs.

Eddie returned to the Storefront Office the next afternoon. Volunteers were hard at work making signs and putting out leaflets. The phone rang constantly.

Josh spotted Eddie and said, "I'm glad your wife told you I called; John Lanington should be by shortly."

"Do you know how Lanington's talk with the Mayor went?" Eddie asked.

"No, I don't," Josh answered. "He just told me to meet him here. Would you like some coffee?"

"Yeah, sure," Eddie said, admiring the busy office.

John Lanington's tall frame slipped through the front door. He smiled at everyone and waved.

"Eddie, isn't it?" he said, shaking hands. "And Josh, there you are. Is there a place we can talk privately?"

They met in the back room. As they sat down Mr. Lazzaro came in and joined them.

"I'll save my ideas for afterwards," Mr. Lazzaro said, taking a seat on a shaky old office chair. "I'm eager to hear what the Mayor is up to."

Lanington sighed deeply.

"After speaking with the Mayor, I don't think we'll be able to convince him to change his mind. He has his heart clearly set on redeveloping the area."

"It's hard for me to believe he would have all these people move out. It's so immoral," Josh argued.

"You've got to realize, the Mayor's a very determined man. He wants the taxes that will come along with the redevelopment of this area. I explained to him it was unjustifiable to tear down the whole West End. He's convinced it is justifiable and that it is in the City's long-term interest."

"I guess you heard by now what happened to us in court the other day," Eddie brought up.

"Oh yes, I got a call from Josh. The Mayor seemed to know about it too. He wasn't too pleased, I can tell you," Lanington said laughing.

"But what about the legality of the City collecting rents?" Eddie questioned.

"Oh yes, it is technically illegal, I believe," Lanington said. "You should withhold your rents. It's the only protest I see available to you at this time. The City would have a difficult time evicting nine thousand residents for not paying."

"It almost sounds like you don't think we have a chance," Eddie surmised.

"No, I'm not saying that," Lanington corrected. "But the process has gone too far. It's going to be hard to reverse."

"Well, I just can't see giving up so easily. If only we can get the people organized; but that's going to be difficult. They seem to want blood. It's going to be a hard group to contain, especially when they hear what the Mayor told you," said Josh.

Lanington nodded morosely. He drummed his fingers on the desk.

"I want you to know that I did all I could. I wish I could offer you a more optimistic outlook," he said as he glanced at his watch. "I've got to go. I'm meeting with one of my colleagues before catching a plane for Washington. I'll see if there's anything I can do down there while I'm working on this legal case my firm is handling."

He stood up and shook hands all around before leaving.

Afterward, everyone looked at one another in disbelief, their faces filled with discouragement.

"Well, he tried," Josh said.

"Sure, sure," Eddie said. "Everybody's trying their best, but where in tarnation is it getting us?"

"Now, now," Mr. Lazzaro said. "Patience, patience. You know, I was just watching that TV of mine the other day and I got an interesting idea. Let me tell you about it."

14
SHAME

On a warm May day Eddie waited in the outer room of the site office, the trailer across from their storefront campaign. He and Mr. Lazzaro were about to enact the plan Mr. Lazzaro had conceived in April. Several other local residents, mostly older and worried, fretted in the waiting room with him. He hadn't seen Angel yet, just his underlings who bustled about and kept them waiting.

Finally a pale man with a skinny black tie and plastic pocket protector filled with pens called Eddie into a cubicle. The man kept his eyes lowered while he scribbled a note.

"Excuse me," Eddie said. "I'd like some help in relocating a neighbor of mine."

The clerk didn't look up at him. He grabbed a blank form and asked. "What's your address?"

"Eight Bulfinch Street."

He printed the address in neat capital letters. Still not looking at Eddie, he said, "Have you filled out this questionnaire?"

"No, what's it for?" Eddie asked.

"To find out what housing you are eligible for," the clerk answered.

"Like I explained before," Eddie said with a grim smile, "it's not for me. It's for a neighbor."

The clerk finally looked up and seemed to focus in Eddie's direction.

"Then why doesn't he come down here himself?"

"He's elderly, okay? I'm helping him out. Is this hard to grasp?" Eddie said.

The man sighed and wrinkles swept over his brow.

"Okay, here, take this form and fill it out. Then go to cubicle C and see the site officer."

Eddie went out in the lobby and filled out the form. He took it down to the site officer who looked like a twin of the first clerk, except he was heavier and sleepier.

Eddie sat in a chair next to the desk as the site officer looked over the form and whistled in frustration.

"This doesn't compute. Who are you? Joseph Lazzaro or Eddie Sveglio?"

"I'm Eddie Sveglio. I want to look at some apartments for Mr. Lazzaro."

"I see, you're helping him out."

"Yes," Eddie said calmly, sounding his rational best.

"Well, I think he's eligible for public housing because of his age, and I see he only has income from part-time work. You're not eligible though, you realize?" the site officer said finally glancing at him.

"Oh, that's okay. I have plans," Eddie said. "Just make sure you give me some good choices."

"Well actually, you're one of the first to come in," the site officer said, shaking his head. "Your friend will have the cream of the crop. A lot of these people are scared. It's good to see people are starting to take us seriously."

"Oh, we do," Eddie said. "Believe me, I'm taking this very seriously."

"That's good," replied the site officer, scribbling down several addresses. "Here...and let us know if your friend decides to take one."

"Oh, you'll be hearing from us. You can count on it." Eddie smiled confidently as the officer waved him out of his cubicle.

Eddie and Mr. Lazzaro approached the old dilapidated building which had an "Apartment for Rent" sign in the ground floor window. Following closely was Laura West, a TV newswoman and her cameraman. Eddie stopped on the front stoop and studied the referral card to make sure he had the correct address.

Then they entered the building's dingy hallway where garbage was strewn about. A mangy white cat scurried through a hole in the wall. A man and woman, looking a lot like a pimp and his prostitute, walked down the stairway.

"Hey, what's this?" the man asked. He looked worried.

"We're looking to rent an apartment," Eddie responded. "Who do we talk to?"

The prostitute pointed to one of the doors.

"Right there is where the super and his wife live."

Eddie knocked on the door. A woman wearing a dirty pink bathrobe opened the door. A cigarette dangled from the corner of her mouth.

"What is this, some kind of survey?" she asked when she saw the camera.

Eddie smiled brightly. "Oh no, we'd like to see the apartment you have for rent."

"You from the West End?" she wanted to know.

"Yes, that's right," Mr. Lazzaro confirmed.

"You know," the woman said, scratching her arm, "a few other people have been referred from that site office where we placed our ad. We just rented one of our apartments to some West End people, but, don't worry, we still have one left. My husband will show it to you."

She leaned back and yelled into the depths of her apartment. "Fred! Fred! Jesus, that guy, you can never find him when you can make a buck! Just a minute, I'll be right back."

Laura , the news journalist, told her cameraman to stop filming.

"Wow, this is a real dump," she remarked. "They can't be serious sending elderly citizens out here."

"Yes, I'm afraid that's just what the Mayor has in mind," Eddie said. "We want you to tell everyone about this."

The woman returned to the door. "I'm sorry. Fred said he already rented the apartment."

"We're not interested anyway," Eddie admitted. "Come on everybody, we'll check out the public housing."

The woman stepped back and slammed her door in their faces.

Mr. Lazzaro and Eddie, followed by Laura and the camera crew in their van, took a cab to the public housing project. The long rows of brick buildings looked like old military barracks. Patches of brown grass and dirt separated the units. They found the superintendent who was most pleased to show off his apartments for television.

The building inside was cold and sterile, concrete block and steel. The superintendent was himself an elderly man who had difficulty climbing the stairs to the third floor. Wheezing up to the final landing, he turned to Eddie and asked, about Mr. Lazzaro. "Say, he's eligible to live here, isn't he?"

"Well yes, the site office said so," Eddie replied and winked at Mr. Lazzaro who nodded yes.

"Good," the skinny little man said. "You know, it's a sad thing taking down that whole area."

"Yeah, we're all unhappy about it," Mr. Lazzaro said.

"A shame, isn't it?" the man said, pausing before a dented metal door. "Well, here we are."

He inserted a master key in the lock and pushed against the steel door.

"What you'll like about this is it's very quiet up here." He looked at Mr. Lazzaro. "I know you'll like that."

"Well, actually, I'm used to noise," Mr. Lazzaro said, walking around the apartment. "We have lots of people, lots of life in my building."

"You can see it's been freshly painted," the superintendent pointed out. "You never have to worry about heat. It's all central."

Mr. Lazzaro scanned the windows and white walls. The space was as sterile as a hospital room.

"Electricity is included with the rent," the superintendent added, continuing on with his tour.

Mr. Lazzaro's face was expressionless. He walked to a window in the kitchen and peered out at a section of expressway and a salvage yard. Eddie stood beside him and studied the scene.

"And there's plenty of space," the super said, opening and closing cabinets.

"Where are all the people?" Mr. Lazzaro said quietly.

"Excuse me?"

"I don't see any people. Where are the stores?" Mr. Lazzaro inquired.

"Oh, we have them up the street. About two blocks up there's a big supermarket."

Eddie didn't want to be angry with the super. He was just doing his job. He looked at the reporter, who was scribbling a note.

"You got enough for a story?" he said, looking at Laura.

Laura nodded and shook her head in dismay.

"I've got plenty for the six o'clock news," she said.

"Good, good," Mr. Lazzaro said. He took the superintendent by the arm and shook his hand. "You have been very kind, sir. We thank you for the tour."

"Well, anytime, mister," the super said. "You planning to rent here or not?"

"Ah, well, we'll think about it and get back to you," Mr. Lazzaro replied. "Thank you for your time. It's been very enlightening."

"Hey, and remember this," the superintendent continued, "there are plenty of people your age around here. Be sure and keep that in mind. " The super followed them down the stairs.

"I'll try to keep that in mind," Mr. Lazzaro said, winking at Eddie.

That evening, Josh and Eddie, along with Anna, Catharine, and other tenement residents, crowded into Mr. Lazzaro's apartment to watch the 6:00 news.

Laura had done magic with the film footage, capturing shots that drove the truth home about the relocation of the West End's older citizens.

Mr. Lazzaro opened several bottles of his homemade wine, and glasses were raised in a toast. Amid laughter and high spirits, people made their way home after the celebration.

"That was a great idea," Eddie told Mr. Lazzaro, as he said goodbye for the night. "That should hit the Mayor where he hurts— potential votes all over the city, especially the elderly vote, huh?"

"Oh yes, it should have quite an impact," Mr. Lazzaro agreed, trying to hide his worry in his voice. "It's a very serious thing, Eddie. Old people...most don't have the power to change things."

"Well, we've made a great sneak attack," Eddie said. "I can't wait to hear their reaction."

"By tomorrow," Mr. Lazzaro said, "we should hear something, something very angry perhaps."

The next day, Eddie and Mario drove a sealed truck down to Providence and left it in a warehouse. No passwords, no trouble. Eddie was unnerved by how easy it was.

Mario looked at him.

"Look at you. You're worrying yourself sick," Mario said as they headed back to Boston. They drove a Chrysler Imperial which they were returning to Buddy at The Club. "I'm just driving vehicles back and forth, doing a little exchange work, as it were, and you're riding shotgun. Hey, Julia's being nice. She'll get her money's worth."

Eddie nodded. He looked out at the little towns they were passing through in southern Massachusetts. *Maybe,* he thought, *maybe I could live out here.* It looked like postcards from a vacation to the country. How could anyone stand all that nothing, totally alien, like the moon. Still...

When he got home, Anna told him to call the Storefront. Josh had called several times and Mr. Lazzaro had stopped by looking for him. Something about the television show.

Anna looked at Eddie and chewed her lower lip. Her face flushed with color.

"What do you and Mario do on those errands?" she asked point blank.

"Nothing much," he said. "We drove a truck to Rhode Island and took a car back. That was it."

Anna looked like she had more to say, but Eddie ignored her and called Josh. The phone was busy. He waited a few minutes, sitting in the hallway, staring at the old photo of his father. He was in his Army uniform wearing a big cocky smile...just months away from his death. He never looked back in fear. How Eddie wished he could remember him, but he had only been a very young child when his father died. Eddie tried the number again. Still busy. He kissed Anna and Catharine quickly and ran down to the Storefront Office.

Josh waved him into the back room.

"Where the heck have you been all day? Angelino wants a powwow. Come on, Mr. Lazzaro's back here in the office."

Before leaving to meet Angel, they spent a few minutes talking about the best way they could confront him. Then Eddie and Mr. Lazzaro took the list of apartments the site officer had given Eddie, and went across the street to the trailer to see Angel.

"I understand Mr. Angelino would like to see us," Mr. Lazzaro said to the receptionist. She made a call and asked them to take a seat. Within a few minutes, the portly site officer Eddie had met before, stepped in and waved them to follow. They went through the cubicles and stepped through a door. In the back of the trailer was Angel's office. Angel, who was on the phone, motioned for them to take a seat.

"We'll take care of it, Mr. Mayor. I've got them here right now. Yes sir, you bet," Angel said, carefully hanging up the phone.

Angel smiled at them and then asked the site officer to stay in the room.

"Well, you've had your little game," Angel acknowledged. He looked at the site officer and then continued again. "That was quite a performance...Are these the two gentlemen who requested the apartment referrals?"

The site officer pointed at Eddie. "Just this one."

"You know if you have a complaint about referrals, you have every right to complain right here to Mr. Espers, our site officer. He's an expert on City properties," Angel added, while adjusting his tie. Angel's Harvard diploma was posted on the paneled wall behind him. A redevelopment map was next to it, with the West End traced in red ink.

"Yeah, just what's the issue here?" Espers said, frowning at the two troublemakers.

"You like playing principal, Angel?" Eddie asked with sarcasm. "I feel like I'm headed for detention."

"Why don't you tell Mr. Espers your problem," Angel suggested, rocking forward in his office chair.

"I'll tell you what the problem is. It's about the apartments you sent me to look at," Eddie said. "The first place was a dump. Don't you people check these places out?"

"No. We don't have the time to check out all the listings we get," Espers said.

"Don't you think you'd better find the time?" Eddie asked. "I thought your job was to help people find a decent place to live. The first place you sent us to was a slum. They should tear that area down and forget about the West End. I think all the slumlords are sending you listings 'cause they know the West Enders don't have any other choice but to live in their shacks."

"We try to do the best we can," Espers emphasized.

"That'll be all, Mr. Espers," Angel said. "I'll handle this from here. Thank you."

Espers went out, shutting the door behind him.

"You know," Angel said, "he's absolutely right. We are doing our best."

Mr. Lazzaro spoke for the first time. "You know, Angel, it was horrible. You saw the TV news show. You shouldn't send old people to such places. It's a shame."

"Look, I'm sorry the apartment wasn't adequate," Angel apologized, pointing to a basket. "See that mess. It's all new apartment listings which have not yet been filed. How can we possibly have the time to check all those out? We're just too busy. You see the size of my staff out there."

"The City could hire more people," Eddie said, "or are the residents less important than the clearing and rebuilding?"

"Please," Angel responded. "You can't think that. We're not evil, and besides, public housing isn't that bad in Boston!"

"Oh, that was great," Eddie said. "Sure, it was quiet, clean, freshly painted...just beautiful. Hell, it looked like a morgue! There's no neighborhood, nothing!"

"Angel," Mr. Lazzaro said, "we don't want to move. The community will do everything legally possible to stop this. We have no choice."

"I don't buy that one bit," Angel said. "You've all known this was coming for years. I'm sorry about it, but there's nothing to do now but make the best of it."

"It's not going to happen," Eddie said. "You're on the wrong side of this one, Angel. You've been bought off."

"Eddie, I'm getting more than a little tired of your accusations and bullying. Evidently, there's nothing I can do for you. And Mr. Lazzaro, you are fortunate to be eligible for public housing."

Mr. Lazzaro stood up. "Let's go, Eddie. There's nothing more we can do here today."

"You think he's fortunate to get public housing? You go live in it," Eddie said to Angel. "What did they do to you over at Harvard? You got ivy for brains now? The City just took over his home, then they offer him public housing that looks like death warmed over. If you can't offer people decent housing, then you should let them stay where they are. You got your head and your career up your butt, pal."

Angel stood up, went round, and opened the door to his office. A big cop was standing just outside in the next office with the site officer.

"Like I said, I don't believe there's anything more I can do for you," Angel said, and pointed them through the door.

Eddie stood his ground by the desk. "You're right, Angel," Eddie shouted. "You can't do anything for me. Come to think of it though, I'm glad you sent us to those other areas. Now I'm convinced I'm not going to move out. And as far as that pile of listings, I'll show you what to do with them. Eddie picked up Angel's wire basket filled with documents, and poured the contents into the wastepaper basket.

"Officer," Angel said. "You want to show these gentlemen out please?"

He stood back as the cop entered the office and ushered them down the corridor to the outside.

"Oh, and by the way, Eddie," Angel said. "Keep your hands off Tony and my cousin, Jenny. Getting tough isn't going to save you or this community."

At the door, Eddie turned to say something to Angel, but the cop gave him a shove in the back. Eddie twisted around, but the cop manhandled him through the door.

Outside the trailer, a *Globe* photographer snapped a shot of "Eddie Sveglio exiting the trailer under police escort"—so read the caption in the morning edition. Eddie was an immediate celebrity in the West End.

Joe Angelino went on TV that evening, answering questions for the news team he had called to his trailer office. He took them on a walking tour, pointing out the so-called "degraded tenement properties" as well as a few others which had already been abandoned by "sensible citizens."

He smiled handsomely for the cameras and talked at length about the West End's fate.

"Is this inevitable, Mr. Angelino? The erosion of ethnic communities like your own, sir?" the reporter said, sticking a microphone in his face. Angel stood before a row of shops and a small playground.

"Oh, sadly, yes, it's a classic pattern," Angel said, gesturing with a wave of his hand. "These areas are mere reminders of a generation that first came to America. Now their children and grandchildren are moving on out *and* up. It's really a matter of us joining the middle class, mainstreaming, finally becoming real Americans. It's painful, but historically typical of Western European immigration patterns. My transition team and I are here to make that process as painless as possible."

"Well, you've clearly got your work cut out for you," the reporter said, as the camera panned to a crowd of nearby protesters. Eddie and Mario were there with signs that said: *Save Our Neighborhood. Stop*

Eminent Domain.

"Yes, we do," Angel said. "But we have the City, State, and Federal agencies fully behind us, and many West End citizens are beginning to accept the inevitable. Really, it's for the best."

15

HARBOR FISHING

In June, early one Sunday afternoon, Luigi visited Mr. Lazzaro in his apartment. The old friends sat together on the couch in the parlor, drank wine, and conversed in Italian.

"You know, Joseph, this is good wine. The older it gets, the better it tastes. Just like my boat—the older she gets, the better she runs."

"Yes, yes," Mr. Lazzaro said.

"You haven't come to work the last few days. Where have you been?" Luigi said.

"Well, my friend, you see the papers, you watch TV...I've been protesting. Eddie and me have been causing some trouble for the City. Last month we pretended to look for apartments."

"Ah, I don't keep up with that box," Luigi gave the TV in the corner a baleful eye. "Did you find something to rent?"

"No, I don't want to live in any other place. This is my home," Mr. Lazzaro said.

Luigi frowned and changed the subject. "Say, I have a good idea. We haven't been fishing for a long time. How about tonight after supper?"

"Maybe."

"It will do us good. Make us forget," Luigi insisted.

"I can't forget," Mr. Lazzaro said. "It isn't right to scatter the community to all four winds. It pulls the heart out of a man to lose his home and his friends. The place where you live your life is the place where you want to die."

There was an uncomfortable silence. Luigi struggled to find something to say.

"Come on, Joseph. We'll find another place. It will be like old times. Anyway, they'll start at the lower end. It will be years before they make it up here."

"No, my friend," Mr. Lazzaro disagreed. "The City is moving quickly now. Three years they say, and complete rebuilding."

"Well, we'll go fishing tonight. I'll be back for you later," Luigi said, setting down his wine glass on the table. "I won't accept no for an answer."

At dusk, Luigi and Mr. Lazzaro stood on the deck of Luigi's small fishing boat as it putted across Boston Harbor. A St. Anthony medal and cross adorned the bow. The boat slid through the shadow of a huge ocean liner and emerged into the sunlight of the main channel.

Luigi expertly cruised through the islands until he found his favorite fishing beds. There he shut down the engine and dropped anchor.

Within ten minutes their baited hooks were tempting the schools of fish passing far below them. They sat back in chairs with their feet propped up on the side looking out at Boston's skyline.

After a long silence, Luigi said in Italian, "I'm glad you're out here, Joseph. All these problems are weighing you down. You worry too much. Eddie...I can see he's bothering you. Acting up. I hear the talk."

"And Joe Angelino too," Mr. Lazzaro interjected.

"I remember when they were little boys, both living in the neighborhood together. It's like a fight between brothers, but you don't have to worry. You're not their father."

Mr. Lazzaro sighed and looked up at the summer sky. "Do you know, Luigi, that ten miles from here, far away in the sky, there are no clocks, no time, no nothing?"

"I never thought of that before," Luigi said, looking heavenward.

"It's quiet here, so quiet. The water looks nice, so peaceful," Mr. Lazzaro said.

"Well, don't let it fool you," Luigi replied, looking out to sea over his shoulder. "A storm can catch you quickly out here."

Suddenly a fish hit Mr. Lazzaro's line. He felt the powerful pull and saw the line zigging and zagging through the surface.

"Hey, you've got a good one," Luigi shouted, looking over the rail. "Give it some slack...okay...okay, now reel it in slowly."

With Luigi coaching him, Mr. Lazzaro struggled and slowly overcame the fish's forceful resistance. Near the surface Luigi spotted it and got the gaff ready.

"It's a blue fish," he shouted with excitement. "Maybe twenty-five pounds. Beautiful!"

"What a fighter," Mr. Lazzaro said as he pulled the flopping fish onto the deck. They grasped it and held it down. Luigi carefully removed the hook from its jaw. It was bleeding only a little and its eye seemed to glare at them defiantly.

"This fella has plenty of dignity. What a good battle he gave you," Luigi said, patting the fish along its glistening side. "What do you think?"

Mr. Lazzaro did not hesitate. He grasped it firmly, avoiding the dorsal fin, and dropped it into the ocean. It hesitated, almost seeming to acknowledge the two men, then whipped its tail fin, and disappeared into the blue depths.

When Mr. Lazzaro's eyes met Luigi's, they were greeted with a warm, understanding smile.

16

TWO WOMEN

The tension on the streets was continuing to build in the West End. Summer had drawn to a close. It was the end of September, and more residents were moving out to the suburbs and surrounding cities. Eddie was growing increasingly frustrated with the slow progress of the Storefront movement.

Mr. Lazzaro and Josh were losing their grip over people's imaginations. So many had already left, and it was very difficult to sustain the hope of those who had stayed behind. The West End began to take on the atmosphere of a besieged city as new capitulations occurred daily.

After she put Catharine to bed and washed the dishes, Anna went into the living room to talk to Eddie.

"My parents have rented the place in Medford," Anna informed him. "They found it today and took the house right away. It's a whole house, Eddie, and there's space enough for the three of us if we want it."

Eddie said nothing. He crossed his arms and was silent.

"They don't want any trouble. They see the handwriting on the wall, and I do too, Eddie," she tried to get him to see her point of view.

"Oh yeah, really?" Eddie replied sarcastically. "You're getting chicken like your parents?"

"Don't be silly. It's practical. Haven't you heard about the gangs that are running around in empty tenements already?" she asked.

"Those are just teenage punks, kids we can track down," Eddie said. "The trouble is, people are yellow. They don't stand and fight. They run like cowards."

"Who's the 'we' that will take care of these problems? Julia and her gang at The Club?" Anna asked.

Eddie looked at her angrily. "Leave the Club and Julia out of this. At least they aren't quitters."

"Oh, sure," Anna said. "Well, I guess your girlfriend thinks of me as a quitter too. She called here today and wants you to reach her at The Club."

Eddie was furious, first with Anna and now with Julia. "I told you before, Anna. I'm not giving up this battle. We can win this...."

"Maybe, Eddie," Anna said with a quiver in her lip. "But I've never seen you like this before. I never knew you until now. You're so angry over this...."

"Good God, Anna!" Eddie hollered. "You just don't get it, do you?"

"No, I don't, Eddie. You're so mean now. You're acting so crazy...I'm afraid of you!"

Anna held her breath as she looked at Eddie with frustration.

"That's it!" Eddie said. "You wanna run? Like I said before. Hit the road! Run away with your parents."

"I just may do that!" Anna shouted back, facing him in the living room. "At least they care about me. At least they still love me!"

Eddie felt his mind flip over into a raging blackness.

"Do what you got to do, Anna," he said, jabbing his finger at her. "Give up on the West End and you're out of my life!"

He grabbed his keys from the hallway bureau and stormed out, slamming the apartment door. Anna collapsed on the sofa and wept.

Eddie went directly to The Club and had a few beers and bet on several races. He told Buddy to let Julia know he was around. Mario pulled him aside and introduced several of the men Eddie had spotted at the auditorium meeting. They were the loud ones who wanted direct action on the streets. Old man Tocci had sent them over to bolster The Club's personnel and protect the territory.

"You're moving up in the organization," Eddie said to Mario.

"Who, me? I'm just an errand boy," Mario said, winking. He adjusted his new gray silk tie. "You have any problems with Joe Angelino, just give a yell...."

Julia called Eddie and asked him to come over to a table in the corner. She was in a business mood. They sat quietly for a moment. She seemed agitated about something. Eddie had a hard time concentrating on the notes she was scribbling about driving schedules and other jobs for Mario and him.

"What's your problem? You becoming such a big community hero you can't focus on your work?" Julia asked, crushing out another cigarette. "Here, let's have a drink."

Eddie didn't object and she raised an eyebrow at that concession. She poured him a stiff whiskey and watched him gulp it down.

"My, my, what's eating you? You were such a clean, straight-shooting married man the last time I saw you."

"Don't call my house again," he said, firmly setting down his glass. She filled it again.

"Oh sorry about that," Julia said. "Well, you've been so busy with your do-good Storefront. I couldn't find you. I hope it didn't cause any conflict."

"Yeah, right!" Eddie said.

"Whoops! I guess we had a little fight at the Sveglio household today," Julia smiled. "Me and my big mouth. I'm sorry, Eddie, really I am."

"Sure, sure," Eddie nodded his head, gulping down more whiskey.

"Hey, take it easy," Julia cautioned, filling his glass again. "This is my father's best stuff...So what did you argue about?"

Eddie was silent, stewing in his anger. "Ah, it's this redevelopment stuff," he said and leaned forward putting his head in his hands. "Anna's parents are moving to Medford and she wants us to go with them."

"Wow, throwing in the towel. No wonder you're pissed off," Julia said. "You know, Anna has never really been a West Ender like us. She was never in our gang, remember? Like I said, I swear I thought she was gonna join a convent."

"Oh, for God's sake," Eddie said. "You never stop, do you?"

Julia giggled. She slid next to him and put her arm around him.

"Look, Eddie," she grabbed his face and made him look at her. "When push comes to shove, who cares about you?"

He stared at her dark, beautiful eyes as she nodded, coaxing him to agree.

"It's the old neighborhood gang. We're like a family together. We look after each other."

"Yeah, sure" Eddie said. "What are you doing to save the West End?"

Julia hesitated. "Well, for one thing, I know my father is making calls. He's pulling every string he can think of. You think he wants to lose this neighborhood? I mean, the West End is only one small part of the business, but we have roots here."

"Well, I haven't seen any results," Eddie complained.

"We're just getting started," Julia responded. "If we have to get tough, we will. Listen, I think what you did on the TV and that picture of you in the *Globe* getting tossed out of Angel's trailer—they, that's great!"

"You mean, you're willing to help?"

"Anything I can do, I'll do," Julia assured him. "I love the West End. And I still love you."

She leaned forward and kissed him gently on the lips. He moved aside slightly while she continued placing small kisses along his cheek and down his neck.

"No, Julia, you better stop," Eddie said softly.

She whispered in his ear as she continued kissing him. "You know we're the only friends you got. We're the real tribe down here in the West End. And we don't take 'no' for an answer."

She stood up and pulled him up from the booth. "Come on Eddie, let's go to my apartment. There's some business I want to discuss with you, "Julia said.

"Ah, Julia. Not tonight," Eddie contested.

"Just when then?" she asked. "Come on, I want to show you how good the West End looks from the roof of my building. The view will give you some good ideas," Julia said.

Later, Eddie hesitated at her bedroom door, but Julia lured him into her warm bed and kept him through the night. The world felt like it was coming apart, going crazy, the rules seemed to be changing. In Julia's strange embrace, a fear crept over Eddie, a fear that he didn't want to acknowledge. Was it possible that he could lose Anna and Catharine? Was he driving them away? He couldn't imagine his life without them.

17

THE WRECKING CREW

The next morning while a strong rain beat down on the West End, Eddie listened to the forecast on Julia's kitchen radio. Several more days of rain were predicted.

He left her place and went back to The Club. He didn't go home. After two in the afternoon, he walked over to the Storefront and sat in with Josh and Mr. Lazzaro. They were planning a propaganda campaign against paying rents to the City.

"Eddie," Mr. Lazzaro whispered at the end of the meeting. "Anna's looking for you. She's worried."

"Thanks," Eddie said. "I'll take care of it, okay?"

"Sure, sure," Mr. Lazzaro nodded, then busied himself with a pile of leaflets.

By late afternoon, they and the volunteers were out on the streets handing out the no-rent leaflets and buttonholing residents for their commitment. Eddie worked his own street and planned to run in and check on Anna. Then he saw Tony.

"Hey Eddie," Tony said. "I'm sorry you're breaking camp, but what did I tell you?"

"What do you mean?" Eddie asked, handing Tony a leaflet.

Tony glanced at the rent protest message and shook his head in resignation.

"I mean Jenny and I are moving to the North End and now I hear you and Anna are moving to Medford with her parents. I guess you've had a change of heart."

"Not at all!" Eddie clarified. "I'm not moving anywhere."

Tony looked puzzled. "Well, you know, Angel was very helpful. He made a call for us and located a nice apartment over in the North End. We almost got a view of the water. You oughta talk with him. He's got a lot of pull."

Eddie glared at Tony.

"Well, that's just great," Eddie said. "You get a nifty little apartment because your wife's cousin is on the City take. You don't give a hoot about us. You've got yours. What about the rest of the people?"

"You know, you're really blowing this whole thing out of proportion," Tony said. "I was just telling Jenny the same thing. Angel called and told us what you did over at the trailer the other day. Man, I'm telling you, cool out." Tony handed the leaflet back to Eddie.

"Stay out of my way," Eddie demanded.

"Hey, no problem," Tony said. "What's between your old lady and you, that's your business. But I can tell you that your family is already packing."

Eddie turned and headed away from the tenement. He was afraid he would lose control with Tony again. He went back to the Storefront and called Anna.

"You're going with your parents?" he asked abruptly.

"Yes, I think it's best. Where were you last night?" Anna asked.

"I don't have to answer to you. You leave with your parents and we're finished. You hear that?"

There was silence at the other end. Eddie hung up the phone and sat staring out the Storefront window at the site trailer parked in the empty lot, shrouded in rain.

Josh and Mr. Lazzaro returned and saw Eddie sitting quietly. They pulled him into the back room.

"Well, we've had a solid morning of success," Josh said. "Our team covered half of the West End, door-to-door. Talk about great saturation. Boy, the City's gonna be surprised when nobody shows up to pay rents."

"Yeah, we did good, too, over on the other side of the West End," Mr. Lazzaro said. "How did it go for you, Eddie?"

Eddie was in a near daze. He looked at the two of them. They were innocents who didn't know what they were up against.

"I don't believe we're getting through," Eddie said bitterly. "People are turning yellow and running."

"Who?" asked Josh.

Eddie had difficulty answering.

"Oh, this business with Tony and Jenny," Mr. Lazzaro said, "that's eating you up. And, ah...."

"Yes," Eddie confessed, "say it, Mr. Lazzaro. Anna and Catharine and her parents are leaving for Medford."

"Nooo!" Josh said in disbelief.

"But I'm not going with them...I'm not giving up." Mr. Lazzaro looked sadly at Eddie.

"Don't worry, Eddie," Mr. Lazzaro said. "Anna will come to her senses. She's torn between the choices. She's very close to her mother and father. You should go home and talk to her."

Eddie felt a wave of anger sweep him. "You haven't got a clue, have you, Mr. Lazzaro?"

"What do you mean?"

"You don't get it. This whole legal approach—the signs, TV interviews, lawyers, priests, leaflets, petitions—none of it is working!"

"Hey, come on," said Josh. "Give it a chance!"

"Give it a chance!" Eddie exclaimed. "Wake up. We're losing this God-forsaken war. Unless we get tough, I mean really tough, nobody down at City Hall or anywhere else will believe us. Another month of this Sunday social crap and we're finished."

"Eddie, calm down," Mr. Lazzaro said, looking surprised. "You're upset about Anna. Give it some time."

"I'm all out of time," Eddie jumped up. "I gotta act."

"Well, here," Josh said, shoving a handful of leaflets in Eddie's hand. "Pass these out."

"You do it!" Eddie yelled, throwing the sheets up in the air. He glared at them and swept out of the storefront.

Eddie hurried down an alley and took a short cut toward The Club. Suddenly a squad car cut him off. Two cops jumped out and ordered him to halt.

"What's this all about?" Eddie demanded to know. He had never seen these two police officers before. They were fair-skinned and looked Irish.

"You micks are out of your turf, aren't you?" Eddie said.

The cops grabbed him and threw him across the hood of their cruiser and began frisking him.

"What the hell," Eddie said. They slammed him down again.

"You're a real wise guy, aren't you?" one of the cops said. "You're on our list now, Eddie Sveglio. A real community troublemaker."

"I haven't done anything," Eddie fired back and struggled slightly. The other cop, seeing no one at either end of the alley, pounded Eddie in the ribs.

"You stupid creep!" Eddie said, gasping for air.

"We've got your freakin' number, big shot. You're Tony Sveglio's son, aren't you, punk?" the older cop asked. "Don't look surprised. We don't forget nothing. You trying to live up to your father's rep, huh? Don't even think about it. You and your wop pals down at The Club. You step outta line and we'll bust you all. And another thing, keep away from the site office. The Mayor don't want you punks causing any more trouble. You got it?"

Eddie was silent. The other cop hit him in the ribs again.

"We can't hear you," the older cop said.

"I'm gonna get your badge numbers, you bastards," Eddie warned them. Someone was coming up the street toward the alley. The cops pulled him up from the hood of the cruiser and pushed him into the alley. He doubled over and leaned against the wall. The cops were gone before Eddie could get a fix on their car number. He waited a minute, catching his breath, and then made his way slowly to The Club.

He found Mario, called the gang from The Club together, and told them what happened. Everyone was angry and wanted revenge. Eddie told them to wait until he could track down who they were.

"Somebody better tell The Boss," Buddy said.

"Who? Julia or her Dad?" Mario asked.

"Hey, Pretty Boy," Buddy said, "there's only one Boss, down here. When you gonna learn?"

"Sorry," Mario apologized and shrugged.

"I'll talk to The Boss," Eddie said. "You guys hang loose. Be careful where you go and what you do. It looks like we're being watched right now."

Eddie stayed at Julia's apartment again that night. He was too sore in his ribs to move much. She tried to doctor and console him. He slept half sitting up on the sofa and she stayed in her bedroom despite several pleas.

"I'm sorry about Anna leaving you," Julia said. "But you know, you and I are too much alike. I should have never let you go. I knew this marriage thing wouldn't work out."

"Please, Julia," Eddie said, gingerly adjusting himself on the cushions. "Let's talk about this later. I need to rest now."

"Yeah, you lie still and rest. Take all the time you need," Julia said, thrilled at playing nurse. She swished about Eddie and let her bathrobe hang open as she bent over him with aspirin and water. At last, she settled in her bedroom and fell asleep.

Eddie lay awake for hours staring at the ceiling and wondering what he could do next. Sometime in the early morning hours he finally dozed off.

At 8 AM Eddie was awakened by a loud rumbling noise outside. He groaned as he got up and went to the window. Julia joined him. In the street below a caravan of trucks, cranes, and bulldozers ground by.

"We got trouble," Eddie said, quickly pulling on his pants. "Julia, will you call Mario and tell him to meet me at the BRA trailer?"

"Sure, I guess, but why there?" Julia asked, picking up the phone to dial. She leaned back and lit her first cigarette of the day.

"Just a hunch," Eddie said. He cursed at the pain he felt when bending to tie his shoes. He wanted to get back at those cops.

He eased down the stairs and walked slowly over to the Storefront. Sure enough, the army of demolition equipment was parking in the lot around the trailer.

Mr. Lazzaro, Josh, and other Storefront volunteers were gathered outside on the sidewalk, staring at the monster assemblage. Mario and the gang from The Club were grouped in a tight knot nearby. The rain changed from drizzle to downpour again.

Eddie nodded grimly to Mr. Lazzaro and Josh and walked over to the gang. He felt a volcano of anger and frustration building up. Angel had some nerve.

"Can you believe this, Eddie?" Mario asked. "Looks like the Mayor is getting restless."

One of the gang members pointed to a construction worker and yelled, "You dumb scab!"

"What do we do now?" Mario was worried.

"Come on," Eddie said as he led the way across the street with the gang in tow. "Follow my move."

"Take it easy, Eddie," said Mr. Lazzaro.

Eddie gave a slight wave of annoyance and kept moving into their space. He saw a contingent of police now emerging from the back of the property. Angel was on the steps of the trailer talking with several of the demolition crew.

Eddie walked toward them and all eyes turned his way. He saw the police who had roughed him up. They were grinning, daring him to do something.

"What goes?" Eddie yelled over the roar of the equipment.

"Whatcha mean?" the crew leader yelled back.

"Why so soon?" Eddie asked, looking at Angel, who looked away.

"Hey pal, we gotta start sometime," the crew leader said.

"So, Angel, what do you plan to tear down first?" Eddie asked.

Angel, rain pouring over his face, stepped down from the trailer and walked up to Eddie and his gang. The police and wrecking crew gathered behind Angel.

Angel adjusted his tie and looked Eddie straight in the eyes.

"Listen, and listen good, Eddie. As soon as a building is vacated, we've got orders to tear it down."

"We'll see about that," Eddie challenged. "No one's planning to move out."

"Wrong, Eddie," Angel disagreed. "Right now, I've got half a dozen on the vacated list. I decide when they come down."

"What's he saying?" Mario said as he craned forward to hear better.

"He said as soon as a building's empty, they've got orders to rip it down," Eddie answered. He turned to the gang behind him. "I guess there's nothing we can do about that."

Mario growled.

"Well, let's go," Eddie shrugged. "I guess you've got us licked."

They turned and headed back to the Storefront office. Angel and his crew turned back to the trailer. At the sidewalk, Eddie spotted Laura, the TV journalist. Julia had alerted her.

Eddie halted the gang at the street and huddled briefly.

"Now's our chance," Eddie explained, "if we want to make our point to all of Boston. The TV cameras are here and rolling. Let's take over this lot! Throw the bums out! What do you say?"

A hoarse cheer arose, and suddenly, en masse, Eddie and the gang turned and ran through the site, leaping up on the bulldozers, cranes, and trucks. They shouted like an attacking band of guerrilla fighters as they climbed the equipment and shoved the drivers off.

The cops and wrecking crew tried to pull the West End gang off the equipment. Fist fights broke out.

Men from the neighborhood began to pour into the lot.

"It's a riot!" an old woman screamed as she ducked into the Storefront.

Cop cars began arriving while the TV cameras caught the chaos. Nightsticks were soon flailing. Angel ran about directing police, pointing out the troublemakers. Eddie saw him finger Mario and then he saw the two cop goons from the alley go after Mario with deadly intent.

Eddie jumped off the bulldozer and with the full force of his body he knocked one cop to the ground. Just as the other cop was about to slam Mario with his nightstick, Eddie grabbed the second cop and threw him down.

Mario's nose was gushing blood and Eddie tried to pull him away. The cop on the ground grabbed Eddie's leg, but Eddie shook his foot to free himself. Unfortunately, the cop's big hands held on. Eddie bent down to pry loose the cop's hands when a flash of light shot through his field of vision.

Eddie felt an explosion in his skull. He saw blood spatter against the cop's face and then he felt his legs buckling and the sky wheeling over his face. There was no sound. The last thing Eddie saw was the other cop and Angel looking down at him from a great height. Then the sky went dark, and there was nothing.

18

ANOTHER WORLD

It was like another world, very tight and dark, and he had receded, withdrawn, into this sanctuary, this cave.

And now there were sounds and occasional flashes of light, like distant thunderstorms in the moonless night, and then a rumbling, a quaking....

Voices like sheets of wind breaking over his cave, his secret place....

It was his mother hovering over his bedside. She wrung her hands in worry and reached for him, but he couldn't get loose.

"Eddie," she said, "you come home this minute." He was running down the street away from the gang, after a game of stick ball. The air was cold. The street lights bright. He was running like a horse in a race. Pulling alongside was...Joe "The Angel" Angelino, that lightning strange kid just come up from Providence—and boy, was he fast. But just at the line of trash cans Eddie made a mighty leap and sailed over the finish line.

"Angel, your mother's calling you, too," Eddie's mother said. "Get up here, both of you!"

"Oh Eddie," his mother said, her hands almost finding him. "If only your father had lived, what a difference that would have made."

She whimpered and searched through a closet and brought out a uniform coat, old and moth-eaten.

"I know he's here somewhere," she muttered, searching the back of the closet's darkness. Turning, she cocked her ear for voices. "I think I hear him coming, Eddie. That will be your father. Ah, and here it is."

She came close to him and held before his eyes a gleaming gold war medal that slowly turned in the dimness in front of his cave.

"Go ahead, take it," she urged. "He's coming to see us."

But from the darkness rose a doorway like the opening of a bottomless grave, and through it came a figure of a man.

"I want you to have this," the man said, dropping the medallion alongside the war medal.

The silver image gleamed brightly and lit up the enormous room in which he was suspended. The medals swung together in the heart of a bright sun that swallowed them both. He fell backward into a deeper silence, a swan dive into delicious emptiness.

When dawn came through the dream world, he felt her body against his, her hand clutching his. She was crying and kissing him on the face. Her warm tears bathed his cheek. She smothered him against her perfumed breasts.

"You have to come out of this, you big idiot," she whispered and cried. "What have you done?"

He tried to open his eyes but could not, but he could hear sounds of her breathing. He tried to speak but there was no sense of speech or movement, only her tugging at him, pulling him into her warmth, and whispers. Then...

"Baby, it's your lover. Speak to me, sweetie."

With rageful sheer red sun holding down his body, he heard them fighting, Julia and Anna. He heard them struggling in the nearby darkness, but not within the red planet where he seemed to be imprisoned.

He tried to see them. He called out to Anna and Catharine. For a few blissful moments he had them again, but then their warmth and smell slipped off the edge of his world.

"Come back!" he tried to shout at what was now faint shadows.

And there came a season of silence, and dust windstorms tore at the face of the desert landscape as well as at his hidden sepulcher.

In a tomb, narrow and cold, he waited for the endless solitude to free him. He felt the two medals burning like a distant star in his night of absolute darkness.

"Well, look who's back in the world of the living," the orderly said, adjusting Eddie's bed.

Eddie tried to focus his eyes on the blurry figure and reached up gingerly, touching the bandage around his aching head.

"Where am I?" he asked around a dry, swollen tongue.

"Ah, now that's a good sign," the orderly said. He wasted no time in signaling the nurse and the doctor, who came to Eddie's bedside at once.

"You're recovering from a concussion and you're under arrest in City Hospital."

"When can I get out of here?" he asked.

"Oh, that depends," the doctor replied.

After the nurse and doctor left, a cop came in the wardroom and pulled up a chair.

"Hey pal, you're lucky to be alive," he made it a point to say.

"When can I get outta here?" Eddie asked again.

"Well, when you're well enough, you'll be transferred to the Charles Street Jail. Then it depends on the bail."

"I gotta get back home," Eddie said. "There's a lot to do. What day is it?"

"Ahh," the cop said, "it's Tuesday the twelfth of September, I think."

Eddie tried to calculate the length of time since the fight, but couldn't remember what day the fight was.

"How long have I been in here?" Eddie wanted to know. He felt a tight grip of fear in his gut.

The guard pushed back his cap and picked up the clipboard from the bed's rail. He studied the sheet.

"Geez, look's like at least four or five days, depending on how you count it."

Eddie tried to put the images of the fight together in his head. Angel and the cops, Mario, Mr. Lazzaro and Josh, Julia and Anna, it seemed like he had been dreaming of them running through his long sleep.

"Anything I can get you?" the guard offered.

"Yeah, help me get outta here," Eddie said, as he tried to sit up. But he froze. A sharp pain slammed through his skull and down his neck. It was excruciating.

"Ohhh, God!" he shrieked, and sank back in the pillow. He closed his eyes. He just wanted to sleep, Heavenly rest, his leg twitching as he felt himself slipping over the edge again.

That night, he awoke and demanded some food. He climbed from the bed and walked carefully down the hall to the nurse's station and back—all under the cautious eye of the two guards who watched the prison ward.

The next morning, after putting on his street clothes, he was handcuffed and taken in a squad car to the Charles Street Jail. He went through booking and found himself inked and photographed and slumped in a jail cell, being studied by four other battered inmates.

He slept on his bunk and awoke briefly to eat some soup. He asked to make a call and they told him he'd have to wait until others had been processed. He tried not to think about Anna, or the scene at the site trailer. Where was everybody when you needed them?

Then he heard his name, as if from far away.

"Sveglio, Eddie. You've made bail. Let's go, it's your lucky day."

His cell mates eyed him enviously.

"It must be nice," one of them said. "Might even be worth gettin' your skull busted, huh?"

There was laughter all around.

Then they were opening the cell doors and he was signing papers and passing into the lobby and the bright sunlight of a mid-September afternoon.

"Who paid my bail?" Eddie asked the desk sergeant.

"I don't know, pal," the sergeant said. "I just come on duty and I'd have to go look it up. You really want to wait around for that?"

Eddie shook his head slowly and felt like he had a brutal hangover.

"Must've been a helluva party," the sergeant remarked.

"I wouldn't know," Eddie said. "I never got there."

He walked out on the sidewalk and looked around. He saw no one familiar. He felt like he had gone time-traveling, and had come back only to find time had passed him by.

He felt a wave of panic. A taxi slowed down and he flagged it.

"Where to, buddy?" the cabbie asked.

"West End," Eddie said, easing down in the front seat. "That is, if it's still there."

131

19

HOMECOMING

The taxi weaved through the narrow streets of the West End and let Eddie off in front of the Storefront. Along the way, he had seen moving trucks crowding several of the streets.

The window of the Storefront campaign had been cracked and tape now held the big pane together. Across the way Eddie saw a long line of older residents lined up at the site trailer.

Josh was walking along the line talking with the people. Eddie joined him.

"Hey, old man," Josh said, greeting him with an embrace. "Wow, are you all right?"

"I'll live," Eddie replied. "What's happening here?"

"They're paying their rents. They got more notices. The city is playing hard ball and it's got them scared. Look at what some thugs did to our Storefront window. We think it was some of those wrecking crew guys. Eddie, let's try to convince them not to pay their rents to the City. You want to start at the other end and we'll meet in the middle? You better start at the far end. I don't think you're very popular with those guys," Josh said, pointing to the cops guarding the demolition equipment.

"Mrs. Scaparotti, why are you paying your rent? Didn't you read our notices?" Eddie asked the first lady he approached.

"I don't want to make trouble. I don't want to be thrown out into the street. I'm an old woman. What can I do?" she asked, wringing her hands nervously.

"Yes, Mrs. Scaparotti, I understand, but—"

"What are we going to do?" the man behind her asked. "They've got us over a barrel. Who wants to be evicted?"

"No one will be evicted if we all stay together."

"Yeah, how you going to fight the law? Haven't you heard you can't fight City Hall? Nothing's worked," the man said.

At the front of the line, Josh talked with an elderly Jewish woman.

"Mrs. Moskowitz, don't you know the best thing to do is to withhold your rent?"

"That's a fine thing for you to say. Your family has plenty of money. You have a way out, Josh," she said.

"Mrs. Moskowitz, our meat market business is all we got and that's at stake. You know that."

"Well, if the others didn't pay their rents, I wouldn't pay mine either. Just look at all the trouble in the papers and on TV...I'm scared. I don't want no trouble, Josh," she said, glancing at the cops and then at Eddie's bandaged head.

"I heard all about what happened to Eddie—inciting to riot, assault, and battery...," she whispered to Josh. "You think he'll get off?"

Josh shrugged. "We'll work something out. Don't worry."

Angel poked his head out of the trailer door and spotted Josh and Eddie working the queue of rent payers. He motioned to a policeman and conferred briefly with him. The cop then called to Eddie and Josh. He spoke to them forcefully.

"You guys, unless you're paying rent, you'll have to move on."

"This is still the West End," Eddie said, feeling his anger returning.

"This is City property now, pal. I heard about you. You're Eddie Sveglio. You're the troublemaker down here, aren't you?" the cop said, stepping closer.

Josh pulled Eddie off the lot and they returned to the Storefront.

"Look, tonight's the second big meeting at the Blackstone Auditorium. We're going all out for a battle plan," Josh told Eddie. "It's make or break time."

"I'll be there," Eddie said. "I've got a score to settle with Joe Angelino."

Eddie walked down the street toward home. A few tenements had already been abandoned. He stopped to peer through a broken window of the barber shop, which was boarded up. He was shocked by the speed at which things were changing.

In front of his tenement, a moving truck was parked. Tony was loading in the last of his things.

"Hey Eddie," he said. "I heard what happened. You okay?"

"Yeah, I'll be okay."

"Well, that's about it for us. Jenny is already at our new apartment in the North End."

"Great," Eddie muttered. He started up the steps.

"Hey Eddie," Tony said. "I'm sorry about the trouble. Anna's parents have moved already to Medford. Guess you'll be catching up with them in a few days, huh? Oh, by the way, there's someone waiting for you upstairs."

Eddie turned and looked at Tony. It must be Anna. She must have come to her senses.

"Have a good life, Antonio."

Eddie went up the stairs slowly, passing Anna's parents' empty apartment. The door stood open and revealed the sad emptiness of their rapid desertion. Good riddance. He had never really trusted them from day one.

He opened the door to his apartment and went in quietly. He didn't want to scare her. He noticed immediately how bare the living room looked. She had probably started packing and then stopped. He heard the water run in the kitchen sink and he walked in, prepared for a fight.

At first, he couldn't get his bearings. The figure of the young woman didn't fit. He blinked and thought for a second his vision was blurred from the concussion.

"Anna?" he questioned.

The woman turned around and faced him. Julia!

"Hi, lover!" she rushed to him.

"Mr. Lazzaro wanted to pay your bail money but I beat him to it. I sent one of the guys down there this morning...anything for you, you big galoot," she hugged and kissed him. "Here, sit down," she said, pulling out a chair for him.

"What are you doing here, Julia?"

"Let me make you some coffee and a little food. Anna left plenty to eat."

Eddie was confused. He slumped down in the chair and held his head in his hands. Julia was already fussing with the coffee pot.

"What's going on?" Eddie asked Julia.

"You really want to know?" Julia replied. "You've been deserted. Your so-called wife has left you. Chickened out when the going got tough. That's what's going on." Julia beamed with self-righteousness.

Eddie moaned slightly and tried to get up.

"No, you don't," Julia said, pushing him down. "You sit right there and rest for a minute. I'm fixing you some food, and while I'm doing that, you can read Anna's letter."

Julia motioned to an opened envelope lying at the other end of the kitchen table. She slid it down to him.

"You read this?" Eddie asked. "You came into my home and read Anna's letter?"

"You better read that, sweetie. It's a good thing I'm here to pick up the pieces," Julia said, snapping the lid on the coffee. "How on earth does this thing work? No, don't get up, you better read your letter. You got a choice to make. Anna's made hers."

Eddie shook his anger off and read the letter.

Dear Eddie, I've taken most of what I need to get started in Medford with our new place. I might be back for a few more things, but I can't bear seeing you angry at me. I visited you in the hospital but you didn't recognize me. I didn't want you to come home and not know what happened. You can call me at the number below. We miss you, but I can't live with the destruction and violence and deceit. Your violence is scaring me. It's scaring everyone. Don't you see that? I want a peaceful life for Catharine and me. I want you to come live with us in Medford. There's plenty of room with my parents. I know you don't want this, but it's time we faced the facts. The West End is not going to be saved from destruction. The choice is yours, of course. Catharine and I miss you and love you, Anna.

Eddie sat quietly and fumbled with the pages of the letter. His mind was filled with emotions—sadness, fear, loss, frustration, and anger. How could she just walk out and take his child away from him? Walk out of their marriage and run after her parents?

Julia sat down and pushed a cup of hot coffee in front of him.

"Here, try this," she insisted.

He looked at her trying to take Anna's place. She sensed his confusion.

"I know you're really mad," Julia said. "You're mad at me for being here. You're mad at Anna for dumping you. Face it, you got two women fighting for you and I intend on winning. I'm not a loser, Eddie. I don't quit and run. The West End is my home, my business now, and you and I aren't quitters."

Eddie stared at the letter and back at Julia.

"She's made her choice; now it's your turn," Julia said. "It's a clear-cut situation. Boy, I'll tell you, she and I had a little scene at the hospital—"

"What happened?" Eddie asked. He remembered vaguely from the mists of his memory.

"Oh, I was there at your bedside and in she came with the baby. Oh, boy, I thought the police were gonna have to restrain her. I left, of course. Old Mr. Lazzaro and her Dad were out in the hallway."

"They all came?" Eddie said, trying to remember.

"Oh, it was old home week," Julia filled him in. "And I was the woman in red! I was the 'tramp', as Anna put it. You know, I still think she would make a good nun or maybe even a librarian...Oh, but Catharine, what a cute baby. You make good babies, Eddie," Julia purred, leaning forward and kissing him on the brow. "Oh, hope that didn't hurt?"

Eddie was trying to get his bearings. His anger ground against his thoughts. He stood up and gripped the back of the chair. Julia stood up and faced him.

"I'm not running away," he said. "I don't care what happens now!"

"That's my Eddie," Julia said as she put her arms around him. He didn't push her away.

"There's a big meeting at the Blackstone tonight," Eddie said. "I want to get our gang together and be there. This may be our last chance to make a difference. Will you help?" he asked, looking Julia straight in the eye.

"I'm here to help you, aren't I? Who was here waiting for you, Eddie? You know I'll do whatever it takes," she whispered and nestled her head against his chest.

20

SHOWDOWN

Eddie and Julia led the gang from The Club over to the Blackstone Auditorium that night. Mario was pumped for the events.

"Hey, why not a rumble with those wrecking guys?" Mario suggested to the group, as they walked the short distance to the auditorium. A block away was the Storefront and site trailer.

"Let's take it easy," Julia suggested. Eddie was stewing about what he would say at the meeting and how he would deal with Mr. Lazzaro.

An even-larger-than-expected crowd had shown up. People were milling about in a frenzy of complaints and worries. Eddie took a seat on the stage with Josh, Mr. Lazzaro, and Mr. Warren. Mr. Lazzaro embraced him.

"But how are you?" Mr. Lazzaro asked.

"I'll live," Eddie said.

"May I have your attention, please? Please, sit down," Mr. Warren said, pounding a gavel on the lectern. People slowly took their seats and quieted down.

"I'm really glad to see the large turnout here tonight. We all know why we're here. The West End is being turned into a laboratory for the testing of urban renewal techniques, and..."

"Where's Representative Nero?" someone shouted.

"Yeah, and where's that Washington guy...Lanington?" another voice shouted.

"I'm not sure why Representative Nero isn't with us tonight," Warren said.

Sitting next to Julia, Mario yelled from the back of the auditorium. "I'll tell you why. He's been bought off by the Mayor, just like all the other politicians!"

"I really don't know...," Mr. Warren said.

The crowd booed loudly.

"We've been betrayed," another member of the gang yelled from the back.

"Eddie and Josh spoke to Mr. Lanington. Maybe Josh can fill you in on what happened," Mr. Warren said, turning over the microphone to Josh.

"Mr. Lanington spoke with the Mayor like he said he would. He told us the Mayor is very determined and it is going to be difficult to change his mind."

"That's what we were trying to tell you at the last meeting. You can't fight the Mayor with peace and love," Mario yelled out, while Julia pulled him down in his seat.

Another man shouted from the middle of the room, "The whole thing is a steal— taking the area away from the people and giving it to some guys who paid off everyone else. This eminent domain stuff is crap. Someone's making a lot of money at our expense. There are areas in the city lots worse than this one."

"Let's storm the Mayor's office!" another shouted.

Mr. Lazzaro approached the microphone and Josh yielded to him.

"Now wait a minute. Let's not resort to that kind of confrontation yet. Like Josh said at the first meeting, hold your rents and don't move out. Those are the best weapons we have."

"Forget that bull!" a gang member said to Mr. Lazzaro. "Forget it! We tried it your way last time and where did it get us? Nowhere!"

The crowd was angrier than before. Mario and other gang members who were now standing in the back of the auditorium began disappearing out the rear exit.

Eddie'd had enough.

"I'm still convinced the best way we can persuade the Mayor is to withhold our rents, and...." Mr. Lazzaro tried to say over the hubbub, "and we shouldn't be fighting amongst ourselves. That's the worst thing we can do."

"Sit down Lazzaro! You're old hat!" someone yelled.

Eddie jumped up and took over the microphone. Mr. Lazzaro did not sit down but stood to his side.

"Now, you don't have to insult the people trying to help!" Eddie shouted into the mike. "Listen up!"

The crowd was on its feet and stirring around.

"You're right, in my opinion," Eddie shouted. "We got traitors everywhere—political gangs, the Mayor's office, Nero, the courts, the Church, and even our own people, people like Joe Angelino who came back to destroy the West End. These people are climbing all over us like vultures. Everyone's trying to get his piece off the carcass of the West End and nobody but us cares!"

"Yeah!" the crowd roared. "Yeah!"

Mr. Lazzaro pulled at Eddie's sleeve. "Take it easy, Eddie," he said. "They're near the boiling point."

"Yes, you're right, Mr. Lazzaro," he said into the microphone. "Yes, West Enders are near the boiling point and looking for action...."

There was a terrific roar of approval.

"We should camp on the Mayor's doorstep!" Eddie shouted. "We should picket his home, his office, we should haunt him wherever he goes!"

Another roar of approval came. Eddie felt the surge of mob anger looking for an outlet.

"And we should drive Joe Angelino and his gang of home wreckers out of the West End!" Eddie yelled.

The crowd went wild, stomping and shouting. Suddenly Eddie spotted Mario waving and screaming at the back of the auditorium. Julia and the gang had disappeared, including Julia. Then he heard it....

"FIRE! FIRE!" Mario yelled. "Those bloodsuckers set fire to the Storefront!"

The mob swept out the exit doors in panic and furious anger. Mr. Lazzaro looked at Eddie with an appeal in his eyes. Eddie looked away and ran through the exit doors with Josh just behind him.

When Eddie got to the scene, the Storefront was ablaze and the fire was spreading to the adjoining old tenements. The mob was in full riot with the wrecking crew, the police, and the fire department. Bulldozers, cranes, and trucks were standing amid the blaze.

Eddie spotted Mario and two other gang members splashing gas on the equipment and sparking it up, while around them the battle raged with fists, stones, sticks, and whatever else came to hand. A rock struck a lamppost causing Eddie to look up to the rooftop, where he saw one of the guys from The Club throwing rocks.

"Hey, stop that, watch your aim!" he yelled. Then he dove through the frenzy toward the site trailer. He was looking for Angel. He saw Mario and his team splashing gas under the trailer and on the sides.

Angel appeared on the office steps and pointed a cop at Mario. It was the same cop who had beaten Eddie. He was going after Mario with a vengeance. He slammed the back of Mario's head with his nightstick. Mario dropped like a rock to the dirt.

Eddie turned the cop around and smashed him with a single crushing blow to the face. The cop fell backward and landed on the ground with a loud thud. He didn't move.

Eddie motioned to Angel to come on. Angel leaped at him in a fury and they rolled over on the ground. Eddie's head flashed with searing pain and then he felt an animal rage. He threw Angel off. Angel rolled over and grabbed a tire iron. He jumped up and swung it viciously at Eddie.

"Go ahead, Angel!" Eddie shouted. "Show your true colors— you're a killer."

"Screw you!" Angel said. "You two-bit punk!"

He swung the tire iron again and Eddie, following his thrust, grabbed it from him and pulled Angel to the ground. The tire iron fell to the side as they wrestled next to the burning site trailer.

"You had to ruin everything!" Eddie shouted, pinning Angel down. "You had to burn us out, you piece of trash!"

"You stupid fool!" Angel shouted at him, his mouth and nose bleeding. "It was your guys who set that fire!"

Mario was there beside Eddie, holding out the tire iron. Blood dripped down Mario's face and he was trembling with fear.

"Here, Eddie," Mario cried out. "Kill the jerk. Look what he's done to us!"

Eddie grabbed the tire iron from Mario and drew back.

"He is a lying bug, a traitor to everyone," Mario screamed. "Smash his head, Eddie!"

"Go ahead, Eddie," Angel said, tears streaming from his eyes. "Just do it!"

For Eddie, it was as if time had stood still, with the metal bar hovering in the air, the mob a distant roar, the heat of the blazing trailer a wall of fire. Mario crouched beside him urging him on. Anger rushed through him again, and his arm began to tremble in anticipation of the blow.

And then a woman in the distance, familiar through the flames and smoke, was mouthing something, screaming silently.

As Eddie leaned over Angel, poised to strike, he saw the two medallions spinning from the chain around his neck, the gold and silver medals, and he heard the crying of his mother.

"Do it!" Mario screamed in his ear.

Eddie drew back, and with all his might, he threw the crowbar deep into the inferno which was raging through the trailer.

"What are you doing, man?" Mario shouted.

"I won't do it!" Eddie shouted back. "I can't do it. I'm finished with this madness."

He felt a huge clot of relief breaking free, rushing from his chest. Mario crouched, dumbstruck, by his side. Eddie pulled Angel up and hugged him.

"I'm sorry, man! I'm sorry," Angel said. "I didn't want this to happen."

Julia was suddenly there in a panic.

"It's Mr. Lazzaro!" she shouted. "He collapsed over there!"

Eddie ran off with Julia, and Angel followed them. Mario struggled after them. Mr. Lazzaro lay on the sidewalk near the Storefront.

"I saw him running after you, Eddie," she said. "Then he saw you fighting with Angel. He was choking and couldn't catch his breath. Then he fell."

Eddie tore open Mr. Lazzaro's shirt and checked his breathing. He opened his eyes and smiled up at Eddie and Angel staring down at him.

"I guess," he said. I guess the old heart..."

"Shhh...," Eddie tried to comfort him.

"Angel can you get an ambulance?"

"No," Mr. Lazzaro said, trying to sit up. "No hospitals. Get me home, boys."

One of the cops who had beaten Eddie suddenly grabbed him by the shoulder and threatened to hit him with his nightstick.

"Let him go," Angel ordered. "He's with me."

The cop looked confused, then heard a yell and went off toward the mob, wailing his stick.

Fire trucks were spraying streams of water on the buildings and the construction equipment.

"Come on," Mario said. "I got a friend's car down the street."

Eddie and Angel carefully lifted Mr. Lazzaro and carried him to the car. Julia went with them and they drove quickly to the tenement a few blocks away.

Mr. Lazzaro's breathing was labored.

"You better get him to a doctor," Julia said. "He don't look that good; his color is kinda blue."

"No hospitals," Mr. Lazzaro whispered.

"You heard the man," Eddie said.

They carried him up to his apartment and put him on his bed. Eddie knew his doctor, old Doc Marconi, and gave him a call. He was on his way immediately, like the old days. When he arrived he was soon closed in with Mr. Lazzaro in the bedroom.

While they waited, Julia cleaned up Mario and Angel in the kitchen. Suddenly, there was a thundering in the stairwell. Eddie looked out the door and a flashbulb went off in his face. A contingent of police stood gathered at the door.

"This is the guy," one of the cops yelled. "He's the troublemaker!"

Eddie froze as more bulbs went off and cameras whirred.

Suddenly, Angel was there.

"I'm the site officer for the BRA and you've got the wrong man, officers!" Angel shouted, pushing Eddie back inside and pulling the door closed.

"We've got a man in there with a heart attack. He's very sick and needs peace and quiet. Now, I want everybody back down the stairs and out on the street. Now!"

Eddie, Mario, and Julia watched from the window as Angel pulled everyone out to the curb and answered questions.

"Jesus," Mario said. "You never know how things will turn out."

Eddie looked at Julia and Mario.

"You two got some explaining to do," Eddie said quietly.

Julia started to object, but just then Doc Marconi came out of the bedroom and shook his head.

"My God, he's a stubborn old bird."

"How is he?" Eddie asked.

"Well, he oughta be in the hospital right now, but you know how that is. He's typical old country. Don't trust hospitals."

"Is he going to make it?" Eddie asked, feeling a tightening in his gut.

"He's got a bad heart," the doctor whispered. "He's been hiding that for years. He wants to talk with you, Eddie. I'll be right out here."

21

APOLOGIES

Mr. Lazzaro was propped up on pillows, looking gray and exhausted. His eyelids fluttered open as Eddie sat down by his bedside.

"Eddie...ahhh..." he said as Eddie took his hand.

"I'm sorry about the trouble tonight," Eddie said softly. "I've had it with the fighting. That's it."

"Good...won't work, you know...won't work," he said, smiling slightly and pressing Eddie's hand. "Better to lose with dignity. Your heart is right. That's a victory too."

"Angel and his gang didn't start the trouble tonight. Our side did. I guess anyone can be bought out if the price is right."

Mr. Lazzaro was breathing heavier. "We'll work it out," Eddie said, trying to remain strong.

Again, he felt his hand being pressed, but Mr. Lazzaro did not open his eyes. He seemed to be concentrating on something far away.

Eddie went out for the doctor and stayed in the living room while the doctor gave Mr. Lazzaro an injection for pain.

Eddie pulled Julia and Mario into the parlor, away from the bedroom door.

"I wanna know why the guys from The Club started the fire," Eddie demanded.

Mario looked down and didn't answer. Julia scowled at him.

"You think a bunch of meetings will get us anywhere?" Julia responded. "You want to be part of our organization, you gotta have guts. The guys were just following orders—my father's. You're supposed to be a leader down here in the West End. He's been grooming you to run things down here. This was a test."

"Give me a break," Eddie said, almost laughing. "What West End? You're burning it down for God's sake. This will only speed up the process. It'll be martial law."

Julia cocked her head and gave him a wise look.

"So? Maybe there's something in it for us," she said, lounging back on the sofa. "Sit down," she said to Eddie, patting the cushions.

"I'll stand, thanks," Eddie replied.

Mario eased down on the sofa arm.

"What's your part in this?" Eddie asked, turning to Mario.

"I gotta think of the future too, you know," Mario said, as he glanced sheepishly but defiantly at Eddie.

"Mario's got a future," Julia chimed in, lighting a cigarette and blowing smoke in the air. "He's the kind of guy we need in the new businesses we'll be running."

"What are you talking about?" Eddie asked.

"The new West End. You didn't think we'd let this market go down the rat hole, did you? There'll be more money in this area than ever before. Get with it, Eddie. Today we're doing serious legitimate business—real estate, construction, and of course, entertainment; everybody likes their recreations. Everybody, I mean everybody, is taking a little bite, even two-bit politicians like Nero get to make noise, save their careers, and take a cut."

"How about Joe Angelino? Is he in on this?" Eddie asked, not believing what he was hearing.

"Angel!" Julia said, and sneered. "Angel's happy to have his little paperwork job. You think he got that job by merit? Ha! He thinks he knows what's going on in Boston. They don't teach you everything at Harvard."

"So, you've been stringing me along all this time," Eddie said. "Who the heck do you think you are?"

"I didn't really see the whole picture," Mario admitted, glancing between Eddie and Julia. "I just gotta think of my future."

"You can do a helluva lot better than this," Eddie said to Mario.

"You're unbelievable, Julia. You haven't changed. You're still trying to be your father's son...and you're a flop!"

"Screw you, Eddie!" Julia retorted, crushing out her cigarette. "You're really out of it, you big macho. You like to kick butt and hurt people, and that's what we needed. A strong man with brains down here during the transition."

"I'm retired," he said. "I've taken the cure."

"Screw you! You mess up my life," Julia continued. "You give Mr. Lazzaro a heart attack. Poor man collapses at the riot, but do you care, no. You're too busy being a glorified hero. "

"You're sick, Julia," Eddie said. "You don't care about Mario, me, or Mr. Lazzaro. You only care about yourself. You're a no good user. You never cared about this tenement, or these families."

Julia jumped up and stormed toward the door. "You're a naive, sentimental fool, Eddie Sveglio!" she shouted. She yanked open the door.

Anna was there in the doorway.

"Oh, it's you!" Julia said, looking her over. "There, take him, he's all yours. You deserve each other!" She charged past Anna, who gave her a fierce scowl.

Eddie went to Anna. He took her in his arms and held her for a minute. Finally, he gently kissed her.

"I came right away," she said between kisses and tears. "I just had this feeling something was wrong. Mom and Dad have Catharine at home in Medford."

Mario started to leave and hesitated at the door. Eddie stopped him.

"Hey, it's okay, man," Eddie said. "We can find a better future. We don't need Julia and her games. Stay awhile."

"It won't be easy without her help," Mario said, slumping in a chair. "Maybe I should go to Hollywood, make a big splash. Problem is, I don't know how to do squat."

"We both got a lot to do," Eddie said, tousling Mario's hair.

They sat together in Mr. Lazzaro's parlor and talked things over. Around them were the mementoes of Mr. Lazzaro's life. Eddie spied the picture of his wife, Catharine, shrouded in black cloth. Anna made some coffee and checked Eddie's bandage on his head.

Then the doctor came out quietly. "He's weaker, much weaker," he said. "It's time to call Father Mora. He's asking for you again, Eddie. Better get in there."

Eddie kissed Anna, who had started to cry again. Mario and Anna looked in as Eddie walked into Mr. Lazzaro's bedroom.

Then Anna closed the door.

Mr. Lazzaro felt Eddie's hand pressing his own and opened his eyes.

"Ah, Eddie," he said, his eyes glowing. "I'm glad you could come up today. Your mother said you could go fishing with Luigi and me...out on the harbor...."

Eddie nodded his head. "Yeah, I can go," he said.

"Remember that flounder we snagged last time? Now, that was good eating. Your mother fixes fish just fine. I'll speak with her on our way to the pier. I've been meaning to drop off a bottle of my wine for her."

"That would be nice," Eddie said, remembering the many gifts Mr. Lazzaro had given his mother through the years.

Mr. Lazzaro almost sat upright, then felt his chest.

"Ooohh, must be something I ate," Mr. Lazzaro said in pain. "I can't remember when it's hurt so much."

"Just lie back and relax. You need some rest."

"Before I go to sleep, Eddie," Mr. Lazzaro said, "I want to talk to you, I've been meaning to, for some time now."

"Of course," Eddie said, as he patted Mr. Lazzaro's hand.

Mr. Lazzaro rolled over toward Eddie.

"You know I always keep my promises. I always did," he said. He seemed to be having difficulty focusing on Eddie's face.

"I kept them to Catharine, your mother, you, everybody...I've tried, you know?"

"Sure."

"Catharine and I, we never had children, but everybody here... they're like my family, my children. And you, Eddie, you're like a good son to me. I promised your mother I'd keep watch over you."

Eddie tried to control his voice.

"You were like a father to me," Eddie said. "All those years growing up here. You're like the father I never had."

"That's right," Mr. Lazzaro said, smiling. "Yes, your father would be very proud of you, Eddie. Any father would be proud of a son like you. You have heart. You have always cared about people. You understand that love knows no defeat."

"Yes, I understand," Eddie agreed.

147

Mr. Lazzaro half sat up again and stared at the door. "I'll bet that's Luigi calling. He's got the boat ready to go fishing. It'll be a great day on the harbor."

"Sure it will."

Eddie lowered his head and wept.

Mr. Lazzaro closed his eyes.

"You've made me very happy through the years, Eddie. Thank you, thank you for being a son to me."

Eddie struggled to choke back his tears. His throat ached with sorrow.

"Oh, what do you mean, thanking me? I should be thanking you," he corrected. He clasped Mr. Lazzaro's hand. Eddie motioned the doctor to come in. He was accompanied by Father Mora who then began administering the last rights to Mr. Lazzaro.

Mr. Lazzaro closed his eyes. His face held a gentle smile as his breath fluttered and came to a stop. His hand went limp.

Mr. Lazzaro was on a boat in a fog, but slowly the fog thinned and he could see his wife Catharine on the shore. She was standing under an ancient, gnarled tree.

The boat touched the shore gently and stopped. Mr. Lazzaro stepped off the boat and walked across the beach toward her. At last, smiling, he enveloped her in his arms and kissed her.

Outside the bedroom, the parlor had filled with tenement residents, including neighbors from the street, and Angel, who had returned from his outpost with the police and media.

As Eddie somberly entered the parlor, Angel embraced Eddie once again. He, too, was tearful.

"I'm sorry it's come to this," Angel whispered. "Mario told me what Julia said. I didn't know the extent of this mess."

"We've both got a lot to learn," Eddie whispered as he swallowed hard.

Eddie, Anna, and the others looked through the doorway as the doctor checked Mr. Lazzaro. He nodded to them. Mr. Lazzaro had gone home.

22

A FRAME WITHOUT A PICTURE

A hint of cold filled the autumn air. The maples on the narrow street had colored, radiantly aglow with the bright sunshine. Many leaves had already fallen to the ground, and were being strewn about by a brisk October wind. Little more than a year had passed since Eddie had seen the City's sign being posted, declaring the redevelopment of the West End. Just over a year, and the government had been able to destroy an entire community, wielding its ruthless power of eminent domain to overtake Eddie's home and all the others.

Eddie and Mario were loading the last of the furniture into an old fruit truck Mario had borrowed for the day. Many of Mr. Lazzaro's things were mixed in with Eddie and Anna's belongings. Eddie had been surprised to find in one of Mr. Lazzaro's bureau drawers many mementoes and old newspaper clippings of Eddie's successes in high school sports. In the same drawer was a handwritten will, which left all of Mr. Lazzaro's little estate to Eddie and Anna. They were awed by his generosity. It would be enough to get them started again.

Anna sat in the truck's cab, crying and hugging Catharine, while Eddie and Mario stacked and adjusted the last piece of furniture in the back of the truck.

Mario shook Eddie's hand, then hugged and kissed Anna and Catharine good-bye.

"I'll be seeing you soon, Eddie," Mario said. "So Anna's Dad has a place for you and will help to get you unloaded?"

"Yeah, Casimo is waiting for us. We'll be there with Anna's parents just a few months," Eddie said. "Then we're relocating. You remember those little towns down toward Providence? There're colleges down there, maybe a future for all of us."

"I guess I could get used to the sticks!" Mario laughed. "Thing is, can they get used to me?"

"We'll soon find out," Eddie said, giving Mario an affectionate slap on the back. "Maybe we can run a transport business together— honest freight this time!"

"You better," Anna said.

"Well, I gotta go now," Mario said, hesitating. He embraced Eddie, let go, and walked away quickly.

"I'll be right back. I'm going upstairs to make sure we've left nothing behind," Eddie told Anna.

"Do you want me to come with you?" Anna asked.

Eddie gently touched Anna's cheek.

"No, you stay here with Catharine. I won't be long."

Eddie entered the ghostlike tenement, climbing the stairway slowly. The tenement was hollow and lifeless. It was like a frame without a picture. It felt unfamiliar, no laughter or voices coming from behind its doors, no Caruso music flowing from Mr. Lazzaro's apartment, no scent of Italian cooking.

Eddie walked into his apartment and looked carefully about the barren rooms. When he left the apartment and closed the door quietly behind him, he noticed Mr. Lazzaro's door was still ajar. Eddie heard a ruffling sound coming from within.

Eddie reverently entered the empty parlor, then the bedroom, where he saw a shade flapping against the partially open bedroom window. He pulled up the shade and stared through his reflection in the glass, at the rooftops and streets of the West End.

He knelt down before the window, continuing to look out upon his old neighborhood street. He was flooded with memories: of childhood, of life in the tenement, of his fight to save the West End, of the loss of his home and Mr. Lazzaro. He remembered Mr. Lazzaro's dying words, "Love knows no defeat."

The memory of the funeral came back to him, and he was praying again with the young priest conducting the service for Mr. Lazzaro.

"Earth to earth, ashes to ashes, dust to dust; looking for the general resurrection in the Last Day, and the life of the world to come; through our Lord Jesus Christ, at whose coming in glorious majesty to judge the world, the earth and the sea shall give up their dead."

Eddie could still see the tearful faces of the small group from the tenement.

The priest continued. "And the corruptible bodies of those who sleep in him shall be changed and made like unto his own glorious body; according to the mighty working, whereby he is able to subdue all things unto himself. I heard a voice from Heaven, saying unto me: Blessed are the dead who die in the Lord from henceforth; Ye, saith the Spirit, that they may rest from their labors; and their works do follow them. Lord, have mercy upon us. The grace of our Lord Jesus Christ, and the love of God and the fellowship of the Holy Spirit, be with you all. Amen."

A creak in the floorboards startled Eddie from his thoughts. He turned around, and saw Anna standing in the doorway, with Catharine in her arms. The sunlight through the window gleamed off the butterfly brooch pinned to Catharine's sweater.

"Tell Daddy it's time to go," Anna said to Catharine.

"Da-da!" Catharine called, stretching her little arms for him.

Eddie stood up, making the sign of the cross. He took one last look at the neighborhood through the window.

Anna was crying again. Eddie tried to kiss away the salty tears on her cheek. Lifting Catharine from her arms, Eddie took Anna by the hand, leading her out into the hallway where they were surrounded by an eerie silence. Gently, Eddie closed Mr. Lazzaro's door behind them. Together, they traveled slowly down the tenement stairs for the last time, letting memories slip away.

Outside of the tenement they climbed into the truck. Eddie started the engine. He hesitated; then, taking a slow, deep breath, he glanced at Anna and Catharine and pulled away.

Ahead of them, down the narrow West End street, the truck traversed between the abandoned tenements and their sidewalk maples, leaves now brushed with red and gold. From the blue sky above, a shaft of bright fresh light beckoned through the trees.

ACKNOWLEDGMENTS

A special thanks to Jim Stallings.

www.ingramcontent.com/pod-product-compliance
Lightning Source LLC
Chambersburg PA
CBHW060122260626
47160CB00005B/1984